Laura Caldwell

The Dog Park

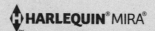

Recycling programs
for this product may
not exist in your area.

ISBN-13: 978-0-7783-1714-2

THE DOG PARK

Printed in U.S.A.

This book is for those who love their dogs
more than just about anything.

The Dog Park

Part I

1

"Jess, enough with this, okay?" Sebastian said in a "weary trending toward cranky" tone. He held out a small bag that read Neiman Marcus. My divorced mind ruffled through a few statements and questions—*What is it? He never used to shop at Neiman Marcus. Judging by the size of the bag it would have to be an accessory. Jewelry? For me?*

But the tone of my ex-husband's voice had pretty much eliminated the possibility that it was a gift. Also, Sebastian hadn't bought me jewelry in a long while, and except for my engagement ring, Sebastian never bought jewelry in the United States. Always it was when he was overseas, on a story. Like the beaded chandelier earrings from a country in Africa I'd never heard of and the vintage Iraqi headdress that I wear as a necklace.

Baxter—our blond, fluffy dog—was in my arms. I kissed him on the head. "I missed you, Baxy," I said. "I missed you *so* much."

He licked my chin, and his butt squirmed as he wagged his tail. Baxy's fifteen pounds of dog against my chest was the most comforting weight in the world to me. When I finally put him down, he tore into my bedroom where he had toys stashed under a chaise lounge, which he hadn't seen in a week while Sebastian had him.

As Baxter rounded the corner, I looked in the bag. I laughed.

"It's not that funny," Sebastian said.

"Oh, c'mon." I lifted from the bag Baxter's blue collar and leash that I had sewn gold stars onto—stars that had come from an old Halloween costume of Sebastian's.

The party had been Harry Potter–themed, and as much as Sebastian would normally have dismissed it as ridiculous, it had been hosted by a journalist he had always emulated. And so Sebastian had been a wizard, dressed in a purple robe with stars and a pointed hat. It's not that he hadn't pulled it off, I just liked to needle him when I could. I also liked the idea of a guys' guy like Sebastian having to walk around with a dog in bedazzled gear. Or maybe I hoped the goofy collar could lessen the pain of our weekly exchange—*Here's the dog back. It's your turn to take care of this thing we both love like a kid, the dog we got when we were trying to keep our marriage intact.*

"I mean, why would you even spend your time doing something like that?" Sebastian asked.

"You know that's what I do, right?" I said. "I'm a stylist. I style."

Sebastian said nothing.

"I don't know why I'm surprised," I said. "It's not like you ever took my job seriously."

"Jesus, Jess, that's not true. Why do you say that?"

"I'm a stylist. You're a journalist. You're the legit one."

"*You're* saying that. Not me. I never said that." Sebastian scoffed and shook his head.

Here we were again—in the ruts of a much-treaded argument.

He pointed at the bag. "That stuff is not what you do with your styling business anyway. You dress people."

"Do you even know what that means?"

Why did I do this? What made me want to bug him, to try and draw him into this crap?

Because it's all you have left.

That was the thought that answered me, and it rang like a bell, a few loud chimes. Then the sound died into the distance, drifting away, just like we had done.

The strong muscles of Sebastian's jaw tensed, clenched. He ran a hand over his curly brown hair that was cut extra short for the summer. "Of course I know what that means. To an extent."

In total, Sebastian and I had known each other for seven years—five of them married, the last of them divorced—and yet we still didn't have a handle on what the other did for a living. Sebastian deliberately withheld, and so I guess I did it, too, in retribution.

"Look, Jess—" Sebastian fake smiled "—we're talking about the collar, right?"

I looked in the bag. "The collar and the leash." I picked them up and jangled them together for effect.

"First of all, look at those." Another shake of his head. "Baxter is a boy. Hell, he's three years old. Bax is a man now."

At the sound of his name, Baxter tore into the kitchen and dropped a white rubber ball at our feet, his tail thumping. *Throw it for me,* I could hear him thinking. *C'mon, throw it for me.*

Like a true child of divorce, Baxter always seemed to know when to deflect the situation.

I picked up the ball and threw it down the hall. He scampered after it, sliding a little on the hardwood floors.

"He's a man who likes this collar and leash," I said, lifting the bag a little.

"How do you know he likes it?"

"He prances around."

"Baxy does not prance," Sebastian said.

"You know he does."

I both hated and loved the familiar feel of the conversation, the verbal poking at one another.

"He's a fifteen-pound prancing machine," I added, another jab.

"He only prances," Sebastian pointed out, "when he's really happy."

"Exactly. And he prances when he's wearing that collar. Point made."

Sebastian just looked at me.

"Anyway…" I said, then let my words die.

"Anyway," he repeated.

A beat went by. Baxter ran into the kitchen again, dropped the ball. He was a mini goldendoodle—a mix of golden retriever and poodle—and the golden part must have had strong genes because the dog would retrieve all day if we let him.

Sebastian lifted the ball, tossed it again.

"Baxter brought something else back," he said, pointing at the bag.

I looked inside again. A white plastic bag was folded over and lay at the bottom. I picked it up and lifted a cellophane bag from inside. "Rawhide," I read from the package. "Huh." I looked at it—half-eaten. I looked back up at Sebastian. "Did you feed him this while he was with you?"

Sebastian raised his eyebrows, gave a slight smile.

That mouth, with its fuller bottom lip. It still got me sometimes. There was the rest of Sebastian, too—the strong body, wide shoulders and long arms that felt so good wrapped around me. But it was that lip most of all that used to get me. I ignored it, looked instead somewhere in the area of his forehead.

"You know that's like giving your kid a bowl of taffy?" I said. "It's completely unhealthy."

"He's got to eat more than raw chicken and raw eggs," Sebastian said.

"That was one week that I did that!" I said. "One week."

I'd been led by our dog trainer to give Baxter a raw diet, lured by the promises of a glossy coat and exceptional health. But when you have your dog every other week, raw foods are hard to keep around all the time. (And kind of unpleasant to serve.)

Sebastian sighed a little and searched my eyes with his. But then he opened his mouth. "I'm on my way to the airport."

Wounds, no longer old, felt jabbed, hurt again. Sebastian was a war correspondent, one of the most well respected. His job had long been our sticking point—his need to go overseas, and his agreeing to not tell anyone, including his spouse, where he was headed. I knew military spouses had to deal with that, but I hadn't married military, and I hadn't re- alized the extent of his investigative writing—the embedding with the troops, the being in the middle of the action.

So he was off once more. I knew better than to ask where he was going.

But apparently he felt some kind of duty to try and make nice. "It's a small conflict."

A "small conflict" could mean a bloody, ruthless

battle in a small Middle Eastern territory. But "small conflict" did not mean small casualties. Sebastian himself had returned from a "small conflict" with a gash across his collarbone that looked a lot like someone had tried to cut his throat. He still hadn't told me what had happened. I still didn't know where he'd been because the newspaper never published his piece for whatever reason.

Baxter ran back into the foyer, a blue earthworm toy hanging from his mouth.

"C'mere, Dogger," Sebastian said. His own nickname for Baxter. He picked him up. "I suppose you're going to the dog park now?" he asked me. I thought I heard another small sigh.

"You know that you can still go to the dog park, right? I didn't get that in the divorce." I paused, made my voice kinder. "I don't know why you don't go when he's with you."

Sebastian shrugged, petted Baxter. "I thought I would find a park by my neighborhood. But they're not the same. He doesn't have his buddies."

I stayed silent. Even when we were together, I was the one, more than Sebastian, who took Bax to the park. And even when Sebastian did, he didn't often talk to the owners of Baxter's dog buddies like I did. Sebastian was intent on quality time with the dog, throwing Baxy's ball over and over, then having him sit and stay for minutes on end before he could retrieve it. He taught Baxter tricks that his father had taught their family golden retrievers over the years. We got the dog shortly after his dad died.

So it seemed obvious to me that Sebastian could continue to do those things in another park. I hadn't expected him to miss the park that we went to, as he apparently did. But I guess change is tough for everyone, even a tough guy like Sebastian.

He stood. "I should go."

I knew better than to ask when he'd return, because I knew the answer. *When I have the story.* That's what he always said.

I used to think, *Why aren't we your story? I want to be your story.*

We had made a plan—move from New York, where we were living at the time, to Chicago (his hometown) where he would work as a regular journalist. It "worked" for a little while. A year or so. But ultimately Sebastian couldn't stop. He couldn't explain why, but he had to be the correspondent who crossed enemy lines in the middle of the night. I encouraged him to let me in. *Keep the job,* I'd said. I'd get used to worrying about him, I'd told him. That was okay. *But bring me into the fold, tell me what you do, what you feel when you're there, how I can support you when you're here.*

He decided that it would be breaking confidences and so he couldn't tell me—not about the stories he was covering, where he was covering them or who he was covering them with. I could read the pieces in the paper, usually a day or two ahead of everyone else. So I would know then, for example, that he'd been in Afghanistan, embedded with a navy SEAL team that took out a top-level terrorist. I would also read the byline and see that he sometimes had cowriters. But he couldn't fill in any blanks. He couldn't answer questions. And if the story had been killed and never published, he couldn't give me any clues. Or he wouldn't. Same thing.

His inability showed me the gaps in our relationship. I had to decide if I could live with the not knowing, the having to make a leap of faith to trust him, when the fact was I knew little about how my husband spent his professional life. And, therefore, much of his life.

I decided I couldn't do that. Or maybe I just couldn't live with the disappointment of not having the kind of love I wanted. I'd thought that with Sebastian I'd had the kind of love my parents had, the kind I'd felt once before. But neither turned out to be true. And eventually, with Sebastian, the ball I'd been pushing uphill for so long started to roll back over me.

Now I looked at Sebastian, said nothing, just stared into his eyes, and some bigger strength kicked in. I was past that, I told myself. I was *way* past it, and I was past him.

I'd started my life over once before. And under

much, much, *much* worse circumstances. I knew I could do it again. I could survive.

Neither of us said anything. But I felt a joint sense of tiredness. *We're done.*

"Okay," I said, just to say something.

When Sebastian didn't reply, the moment of pause gave me time to make a decision. I decided then I wasn't just going to survive. I was going to thrive. I was going to come alive.

Right now. Those words intoned through me.

And suddenly it seemed clear what I had to do right then, how I had to conduct myself going forward. There would be no more seeing life as an endurance exercise. No more considering dates just because a software program told me I should. I wouldn't just react to Sebastian or the lack of him. I would stop seeing everything as a reminder of the lives past. I would open my eyes and see things differently.

I would be different.

"Have a good trip," I said, and I opened the door.

2

After Sebastian left, I put Bax in the gold-starred blue collar, clipped on the matching leash, and Baxter and I took a come-to-Jesus walk. It was the kind of walk we needed in order to get reacquainted after a week apart, in order to become Jess and Baxter again. Such walks were usually long and meandering, often around favorite places like the Lincoln Park Lagoon or the beach, but always landing at the dog park. Once we came back from such a walk, Bax and I always returned to normal. To get Baxter acquainted to the neighborhood again, I first walked Baxter down State Street, cutting up and around Goethe, Burton and Astor, letting him stop and sniff every wrought iron fence and bountiful bush that he wanted. It was a gorgeous summer day, one that was warm but not unbearable as the previous three weeks had been. Instead of huddling in air-conditioned rooms (or coffee shops or bars) everyone was outside. This was the same route Sebastian and

I used to take when we first got Baxter. It was hard not to think of that time.

The decision to get a puppy had been carefully debated, test-driven. We had long thought we'd get a shelter dog. We had volunteered at rescues, had run 5K races to raise money for no-kill facilities. We regularly visited adoption places in Chicago. We dogsat and read dog books and frequented dog parks. In the end, we fell in love with the idea of a golden-doodle (no shed, hypoallergenic) and a mini one. Sebastian pointed out that a dog under twenty pounds could travel with us. *We* could *travel*. That's what he'd said. *We*. And we decided we wanted a puppy, a brand-new being in the brand-new world we were creating. Or trying to create.

So we investigated every breeder. We visited many. We called people who'd gotten puppies from them before. It felt, joyously, like Sebastian and I were working together on one of his stories.

The day we got him felt so alive in my memory, I could almost touch it when I closed my eyes. A responsibility never felt so good before—the responsibility of deciding to take custody of a new creature, a new ball of life energy, and pledging to care for it.

We decided I would take the wheel during the three-hour drive to Indiana. Sebastian would drive the return trip while I rode with the puppy in the back, which the breeder had recommended for bonding.

We'd already been once to the breeder's farm, run

by a young family, with a red barn behind the house. So it wasn't a surprise to walk in that house in the middle of winter and see two litters of squirming golden fluff. But what was different was that one would be ours. *Ours.* I loved that word.

Sebastian and I clasped hands tight as the breeder led us to the eight-week-old litter in the back—six dogs, four females and two males, one of whom was soon to be (that word again) *ours.*

The breeder was in her late thirties with curly copper hair that matched some of the dogs in her barn. She smiled over her shoulder at us. "Ready?"

She opened an octagon-shaped enclosure that held the litter and quickly waved a hand. "Get in before one gets out."

We were rushed by puppies—scraps of panting aliveness crawling over us, their faces peering up at ours, pink tongues darting at our chins.

"How are we going to decide?" Sebastian asked. He laughed then, as a red-goldish puppy climbed up and stuck her tongue in Sebastian's nose.

The hour we spent in that pen was a different world in a different time. We were suspended in between our old lives and our new, and we both knew it.

While all the pups scrambled and licked and nibbled, one boy was a ferocious biter and a jumper. I kissed him on the head. "I feel bad but we've ruled him out," I told Sebastian.

"What about this one?" He held out a two-and-a-half-pound little girl, already sleeping in the palm of his hand. I took her and cuddled her to me, letting her siblings squirm around Sebastian and me, both cross-legged in the pen.

She burrowed into the crook of my neck as I held her up. "She's one of the front-runners," I said.

We played with each of them, trying to be systematic, which was impossible. We came up with names for them to try and keep them separate—Cutie for the sweet, sleepy girl, Biter for the ruled-out boy.

Big Eyes was what we called the other boy. He had an interesting way of observing the group, happy to sit back for a moment when it wasn't his turn and watching the other pups and us before deciding to get back into the fray with a paw to the head of one of his sisters. He was a lover, too, kept burrowing his snout in the crook of Sebastian's knee or under my sweater. Pretty soon, we loved him back. And Big Eyes became Baxter.

But even though Baxter was the best of dogs, beloved by us both, Sebastian and I didn't stay together, and now we shared that soul that we'd adopted.

Baxter pulled hard on the leash, maybe sensing I was lost in my thoughts. As we made our way to North Avenue and he realized we were headed for the park, he tugged even harder, his little golden legs churning.

"Take it easy, buddy," I said, but I smiled. As Baxter's legs churned faster, I could see the images flying through his head—the dog friends he might see, the birds he might chase.

I looked at my watch, hoping the other dog owners we knew would be there. We were people who probably wouldn't know each other otherwise. But our dogs were friends. Odd and simple as that. And so we had roughly learned each other's schedules. And we shot to meet up in the late morning like now.

At this hour, during the weeks Sebastian had Baxter at his place, I really didn't know what to do with myself. Sometimes, I would still go to the park and chat with the others, but I always felt forlorn, rubbing the mini tennis ball inside my pocket, no dog to throw to, always missing Baxter. Sometimes Sebastian.

Although any missing of the ex would stop now, I reminded myself, since I planned to come alive without Sebastian.

We reached the park and, as hoped, some of Baxter's pals and their owners were there. Among the dogs was Comiskey—a border collie named after former White Sox Comiskey Park, but called Miskie for short—and a pug named Miss Puggles. The pug had a historical air about her, one of a heavy, corseted woman who talked in a high voice, always held an aperitif in hand, but Miss Puggles was always social and friendly. Rounding out Baxter's pals in attendance was a tiny scrap of white fluff named Daisy. Daisy must have weighed all of eight pounds, but she had the heart of a German shepherd. She chased after the other dogs, her little legs racing doubly fast.

As we entered the park, Daisy skidded into the sandy baseball pitch after a ball. Then Baxter and Daisy saw each other, and, as always, it was all Romeo and Juliet. Daisy's head raised, the ball dropped, and as she churned her little legs toward Baxter, he did, too—two lovers racing across a green lawn to tangle and nip at each other.

Bax jumped and picked up the pace, making Daisy speed after him in pursuit. I stopped momentarily, thinking how similar their relationship was to Sebastian's and mine—an awful lot of chasing on my part. But that was all done. I reminded myself I would thrive on my own. With my dog. (Whenever I got to have him.)

I walked over and spoke to Daisy's owner, Maureen, who was talking with the British couple who owned the pug.

"Did Daisy go to the groomers?" Tabitha, the wife, asked Maureen.

"We *had* to. She found something dead in our alley and before I could stop her, she flipped over and rolled in it."

"Eew," we all said.

"Thank God Miss Puggles doesn't do that," Tabitha said. "She wouldn't deign to."

We watched as Miss Puggles sassed around the park, heavy-snouted with a light, sashaying rear.

Baxter spun away from Daisy and tried to entice Miss Puggles into playing. Eventually, he turned his sights back on Daisy, and the whole thing started again.

"So you have Baxter back," Al said to me.

"Yeah. I missed him so much."

"I don't know how you guys do it."

He said this to me at least a few times a month.

His wife swatted his arm. "Al, leave it."

"Hey, have you guys ever tried that bitter apple spray?" Maureen said. "Daisy is still chewing the one end of my couch. It's making me crazy!"

We talked for the next thirty minutes about all things dog, from the food we fed them and their digestive systems, to their antics and habits.

The group broke up when Maureen announced she had a lunch date.

"Great. Have fun," I said, wishing I had a lunch date myself. But who did I want that date to be with? I had no idea.

I hadn't met many people since Sebastian and I split up. I'd made a stab at internet dating, but felt too out of the game to make a decision to go out with any of the guys who'd written me. I'd since canceled my membership. I was too concerned, apparently, with picking over the life I'd had with Sebastian.

But now that I'd decided to move on, I should grab opportunities. Maybe I'd go out with the weather guy that my broadcaster friend was always trying to set me up with. Maybe I'd try to date online again. I'd go after business harder, maybe start courting some of the local magazines more so I could style their shoots.

Bax and I continued our walk and when we reached the busy intersection of North and Clark I decided to take Baxter toward the nature museum and the creek behind it.

We stopped for a moment at the corner. "Sit," I said to Baxy. He did so obediently. I smiled a smug grin, thinking, *He is such a good dog. Sebastian and I got so lucky.*

"Hey, Mrs. Hess."

It didn't used to irk me when people called me that. Sebastian was fairly well-known in Chicago and I was known as his wife. So although I hadn't taken Sebastian's name, preferring Jessica Champlin to Jess Hess, I never minded. But now that we were split up, now that I was on my own, it bothered me.

I turned. Then it didn't bother me so much. "Hi, Vinnie."

Vinnie was a sweet fifteen-year-old kid. I'd known him for a few years, since Sebastian and I had moved to this neighborhood. Back then, he went by William or Will. That was his middle name. (Apparently, his parents had named him Vincent only as a tribute to a grandfather who died on the day he was born.) But recently, upon entering high school, apparently in protest to some perceived injustice, Will started calling himself Vinnie. His parents hated it, so he kept using it. He'd told me this one time when Bax and I were at the park and Vinnie was hanging around shooting short films on his phone.

The kid was always behind that phone, videoing something. Often he chuckled, scolded himself for a bad shot or generally just mumbled low, narrating, apparently.

Once he showed me the short films he'd made. Some were silent, with a sort of French feel. Others were loud, raucous street scenes. He seemed to like the juxtaposition of the two. After that, I'd looked at the webpage where he posted his films, and saw he had a lot of followers online. A hell of a lot more than I did.

"Hey, Baxter," Vinnie said. He bent and petted Baxter on the head. Baxter batted his golden tail on the ground.

"How's he doing?" Vinnie said, pointing to the dog.

"Good. I just got him back from his dad." Yeah, that was how I talked. I was Baxter's mom and Sebastian his dad. I was fully aware that I was a childless woman in her thirties whose dog was her kid. (Hence Baxter's winter sweaters that were just waiting to be worn and the fact that I sometimes signed emails to friends, "Jess and Baxter." I wasn't even embarrassed.)

Baxter stood suddenly, his nose pointed across the street, his eyes peering.

I saw a mastiff walking with his owner. (His dad, I mean.) Although Baxter weighed all of fifteen pounds, he often seemed to think he was heavier and wanted to play with dogs much larger than he was.

I considered going back to the park, where it appeared the mastiff was heading, but then Bax strained on the leash even more.

"Sit," I said.

Nothing.

"Sit!" I demanded, pointing at the ground as I'd been instructed by an obedience trainer.

But not only did Baxter *not* sit—he ran. Or rather, he *bolted*.

And not toward the mastiff but horizontally across North Avenue to the opposite corner.

A little toddler, an adorable girl in a yellow dress, stood there with her mom in front of a bank.

"No!" I yelled. "Baxter, stop!"

If there was one behavioral issue Baxter possessed, it was that he not only wanted to play with big dogs, he wanted to play with little kids, a desire that sometimes resulted in him jumping on children, often terrifying both parent and child. Luckily, he'd never come close to biting or hurting anyone and I no longer feared he would.

Until that minute.

Baxter was running fast, and he was headed right toward the toddler.

3

Vinnie, the little jackass, laughed as Baxter ran. Out of the corner of my eye, I saw the kid raise his phone.

"No!" I yelled, not at Vinnie but at the dog.

By then Baxter had nearly reached the other side of the street.

"Baxter, no!" I yelled again.

And then he tackled the kid. Absolutely tackled her.

The mother screamed and lunged at her daughter.

A truck whizzed by. "Baxter!" I shouted, sure he was going to be mowed down.

Instead, he stood over the toddler, panting.

I charged after him, yelling his name.

When I got there, the mother was on the ground, cradling her child. The girl was surprisingly dry-eyed, but the mom was crying.

"I'm so sorry!" I said, shoving Baxter out of the way with my leg but grabbing his leash so he couldn't get too far.

Baxter took a couple steps back, but his panting gaze remained on the toddler. She was a little beauty who was smiling and cooing in her mother's arms, as if she had no idea the quick turn of events that had just happened.

"I'm so sorry," I said again. I crouched next to mother and child, careful not to get too close. The mom was young, wearing white jeans and a pink T-shirt.

She looked up at me, tears rimming her blue eyes.

"I truly apologize," I said. "He's really a friendly dog, but sometimes he doesn't know his limits. That's our fault. My husband says I…"

I shut up. What did it matter what "my husband" (who was no longer my husband) thought about a dog who tackled tots? It didn't matter that we'd gotten the dog to try and stay together, but had lost each other anyway. And it certainly didn't matter how many obedience professionals we had contacted about this jumping problem of Baxter's.

To my surprise, the woman smiled at me. "He saved her," she said. "Didn't you see that? He saved my daughter."

"Good work, Baxter!" I heard from behind me.

I turned to see Vinnie, holding out his cell phone.

"Check this out," he said. "That truck had no idea."

"I know," the mom said.

"The truck?" I said.

Vinnie stopped and looked down at the child and her mom. "She okay?"

The mom nodded vigorously. "Her name is Clara." She held her kid tighter.

"Check this out." Vinnie held out his phone— there was a still image of Baxter dashing across the street, his gold-starred collar gleaming and his gold-starred, blue leash blazing behind him.

"He looks like a superdog," Vinnie said. He fiddled with his phone, then turned it back to us. "Watch this."

He pushed Play. There was Baxter, dashing, the leash streaming behind him. But at the top of the screen…

"See the truck?" Vinnie said, crouching next to us.

I nodded. A white delivery truck. And it was headed right at Clara, who was taking a wobbly step off the curb. "Oh, my God," I said.

Just before the truck hit her, Baxter tackled her.

"Your dog saved my daughter," the mom said. She held out her hand. "I'm Betsy."

I noticed Vinnie seemed to be videoing again, but I was too relieved to protest.

I shook the mom's hand. "Jessica."

"Jessa!" the toddler said in a mumble, mimicking me.

We all laughed.

Betsy, her arms still around Clara, turned to Baxter. "And who is this one?"

"This is Baxter."

I let go of Baxter's leash, and he took a few steps toward Betsy and Clara. Betsy kissed him on the top of his head. Baxter licked Clara's ear.

"Baxter, no," I said.

"Oh, don't worry," Betsy said. "In my book, this dog gets to do whatever he wants."

I looked up at Vinnie. He was still taping our exchange. "Vinnie," I said. "Enough."

"Okay, cool." He put the phone in his pocket. "But I'm putting this online."

Words, it would turn out, that would change everything.

4

The first call came at five o'clock that evening, just eight hours after Sebastian had brought Baxter to my house.

After the incident on the street, Baxter was wiped out. We went home and he slept most of the day. I cleaned the house, returned emails about an Art Institute benefit and read through specs sent by a magazine editor I was working with. It was my first time styling a photo shoot for them. I wanted to do a great job so I could work with her again.

When Baxter finally roused, we took another walk, and I threw a ball in the alley for him.

Really, aside from the scene on the street (which, though scary, had taken only a few minutes), it was like any other day.

The phone—the landline I used for business— was ringing when we walked in the condo. It was Victory, a state senator with a great name, who had retained me for the past six months to outfit her with chic but serious suits and dresses. "Jessica, do you have a dog named Baxter?" she said.

"I do," I said, a little surprised. Although I'd heard Victory mention a dog named DeeDee in the past, with her four children and the political job and being a consultant on the side, she had little time to chit-chat about pets.

"My kids just showed me the video," she said.

It took a minute to process. "Oh, my dog and the toddler?"

"Yeah, your dog *saving* the toddler. The video is called 'Superdog' and with that leash, he sure looks like it."

"How did you know it was my dog?"

"There was a link to a follow-up video, and it shows you talking to the mom. I don't know who put it up."

"Vinnie," I said. "He's a neighborhood kid who shot it." My laptop was on the counter, and I clicked on a search engine and typed in *Superdog.* Sure enough, there it was.

"My kids are in love with your dog. They say DeeDee needs a brother or sister. They also say the video has a thousand hits."

"Seriously?" I peered at the screen. *1374 views,* it said under the first shot—Baxter in full run, his starred leash forming a straight line behind him.

I heard kids talking in the background.

"They want to know what kind of dog it is," Victory said.

"Goldendoodle. A mini."

She repeated my words to her kids. I heard more children talking.

"We are not getting another dog," she said away from the phone. Then in a lowered tone, she continued, "Out of curiosity…where *did* you get that dog?"

And that was the question that also arose in the next call (from a neighbor up the street) and the next (another client) and the next (Sebastian's buddy). They'd all seen the Superdog video. They all wanted to know the story behind it. And then inevitably, "Where did you get that dog?"

I watched the video about twenty times—Baxter a flash as he bolted across the street, a blue-gold streak that became a yellow blur when he collided with Clara, the white delivery truck speeding by a nanosecond later.

I tried calling Sebastian. Baxter was his kid, too, and all that. But of course his phone was off. I didn't even get to hear his voice, because he utilized an automated message, required by his job. He was off somewhere in that "small conflict."

Didn't matter. I was going to enjoy it all by myself.

The next morning, another call—from my broadcaster client, Pamela Nyman, one of Chicago's most well-known newscasters. She now had her own morning show, and her producer had hired me to select outfits to wear on set. We'd kept working together since then and I'd shop for events for her.

"Jess," she said, her voice hurried. "Glad I got you. Do you remember when we were at that store on Halsted? I was bitching about the videos we sometimes have to show?"

"Something about a bear?"

"Yeah. That one was a bear who put his head in a garbage can and got stuck. The beast was stumbling around with the can on its head."

I laughed.

She groaned. "Fine, it's funny, but it isn't noteworthy. Sometimes I just can't believe I have to act interested in it. Anyway, I may be coming around to these videos. I got to work this morning, and they told me we were running one." I heard talking in the background. "We're about to run it now, in fact. And guess whose dog is in it?"

"Oh, geez, is it Baxter?" I got a quickening of excitement.

"You got it. I recognized him from that time we had a dog date." Pamela had a Yorkie who Baxter had hit it off with immediately. "And the video really is adorable. Remarkable. But I wanted to make sure you were okay with us showing it. I can ask the producer to kill it if you're not comfortable."

I thought about it. I should probably ask Sebastian first, but he was unreachable. Anyway, it would be fun.

"Hell, yeah," I said. "Roll with it."

"Great! We're not showing the whole video, like the part you were in—though I saw it. You were running like a mad woman."

"And screaming like one," I said. "This is hilarious. It just happened yesterday."

"That's how these things go," she said. "And that Baxy is damn cute. You'd better get ready."

"For what?"

"Craziness. If you want it."

"I want it," I said without hesitation.

There was a shout in the background. "Gotta get on set," Pamela said before she hung up. "Turn on the TV."

"Baxter!" I yelled. He was in the laundry room, which was his current favorite locale to roll around with the stuffed blue earthworm.

He came trotting out, worm hanging from his mouth, while I scrambled for the remote.

"Watch, Baxy," I said, pointing to the TV and scrolling fast to find Pamela's network.

Baxter looked in the direction of the TV, but generally he didn't seem to know how to focus on it.

He dropped onto his back and, holding the stuffed blue earthworm with both sets of paws, began chewing on its head.

I found the channel and saw Pamela. She was

dressed in a purple dress I'd found for her at Barneys that fit tight to her great figure and highlighted her chestnut brown hair.

"Well, we like to bring you the occasional animal video," she said with a smile (one so good-natured you wouldn't know that she generally disliked such videos). "Usually these are humorous, often they're cute, but it's not all the time we get to see an animal save someone. In this case, a child. Watch."

There was Baxter with the streaming gold stars. There was my voice shrieking at him to stop. And then the speeding truck and Baxter head-butting Clara, knocking her out of the way.

"Amazing," said Pamela's broadcast partner, a handsome man with a helmet of black hair. "That dog saved that kid's life."

"He did. And we've learned that the dog's name is Baxter."

"Baxter, the Superdog," the male broadcaster said.

"Baxter, the Superdog," Pamela repeated.

5

By the end of the morning, I'd had at least twenty phone calls, most from friends or colleagues who'd seen the video.

"My kid loves it!" said a friend from Manhattan. "She's carrying around her phone and showing it to everyone in her class."

The breeder from whom we'd gotten Baxy called, too. "We are getting calls and emails constantly! We don't have enough litters to satisfy them all."

"Sorry," I said.

"Are you kidding?" she said. "This is great. It's the best business we've ever had. We'll just raise rates. And we're sending you a finder's fee for each one who has seen the video and buys a dog."

"Oh, you don't have to do that."

"We have to do something! You've tripled our business in one day."

"Really?"

"Really. You know we're picky about our owners.

We only want people who are really serious about caring for the dog. But yeah."

"So if I think someone's a good fit, and I make them happy by recommending one of your golden-doodles and they buy one, I'll get a percentage?"

"Absolutely. We know another family with a smaller but similar business. They have excellent dogs, and we've been wanting to partner with them."

I remembered the price we'd paid for Baxter and did the math. "Wow," I said. "Hey, thank you for giving us Baxter. He means a lot to both Sebastian and me."

I realized as I said it that she didn't know we were divorced. And suddenly I didn't want to tell her, didn't want her to worry that our divorce caused a lack of devotion to Baxter.

"You know with your percentage," she said, "we could also donate to your favorite charity."

A charitable organization leaped to mind. One I hadn't thought of in a long, long time.

"The Amalie Project," I said. Just saying the words flooded my body with memories. I felt flush with embarrassment, humiliation and ultimately triumph from having climbed out of that space.

"The Amalie Project," the breeder said. "What's that?"

I couldn't believe I'd blurted it out. "Uh…they help women in need."

"Great! We'll give something in your name. Aside from your fee."

"Oh…no, that's okay." I didn't want my name on the donation. My name had been associated with the Amalie Project once. Back in New York. "I'd rather it go to a rescue shelter."

As much as I wanted to support the Amalie Project, as much as it had helped me, I did not want to go back in any way.

6

Labrabullies! That's what Sebastian and I took to calling the two black Labradors who sometimes showed up at the dog park. Their heads were as big as basketballs, their girth like round oak barrels. The owner, a fiftyish guy, usually sat on a far park bench, sipping coffee and working furiously on his phone. As a result, the walk of the Labrabullies was a combination amble, saunter and swagger. They didn't run. They didn't have to. They intimidated. And there was really no one to stop them. The owner rarely noticed until one of them had nearly taken a limb off another dog.

Most dogs dropped when they saw them. They pretended to be part of a tree stump or to feign a stroke.

But not Baxter. Instead, he always trotted around them, orange squeaky ball in his mouth. He did this despite how we tried to direct him elsewhere, how I pulled him into the long grassy area to play fetch, normally one of his favorite activities. And always, the Labrabullies would lunge and snarl at him, try to take away his ball. And yet the next time we saw them, Bax would do it again. He simply couldn't seem to stand the thought that the bullies didn't like him. There was no way to explain to Bax that they were equal-opportunity haters.

So it wasn't surprising when Baxter headed toward the Labrabullies that day he was on morning TV. What was different was his direct approach. Maybe it was subconsciously knowing that he was Superdog that caused Baxter to not just approach the bullies in a circular fashion that day but to charge over to them. Maybe it had been the tackling of the little girl, which he had not been punished for in any way.

"Hey, Baxter!" I shouted. "Come!"

He feigned deafness.

When Baxter reached the bullies, per regular custom, they charged at him, growling. Baxter threw in a sneak move and dropped his ball, then took a few steps back, so they could hoover it. The Labrabully with the dingy red collar tossed it to the one with a gray collar, who ran it to a wading pond and dunked the ball like bread in olive oil, then began to eat it. The red one stood by, ready to take over if needed.

Baxter headed toward the eating bully, while some other dogs moved along with him. Rather than egging him on, the other dogs seemed to be trying to herd him away, to telepathically say, *Let it go, pal. It is so not worth it.*

I ran toward him from across the park. "Baxter!"

Baxy ignored all of us, trotting toward the bullies. Once there, without warning, he swatted the one with the gray collar with his furry paw. A ferocious snarl arose from the bully, a column of hair standing up on his back. The owner noticed for once and he ran, too, dropping his coffee en route, then grabbing one of his dogs before it locked its jaws on to Baxy.

"Sorry, sorry," the owner said to me.

"It's his fault, too," I said, grabbing Baxter and picking him up.

After I scolded him ("Baxter, when I say 'come' you come"), Bax retreated to a bench, sitting under it for about ten minutes. But then he was over the trauma, and he emerged from under my legs, looking around. I thought he was checking out the scene for the arrival of some of his pack —Daisy or Miss Puggles—but when he was twenty feet away from me, I noticed he was running for the bullies. And they were running for him.

"Baxter!" I yelled. "Come!"

I heard the Labrabully owner swear. "Damn it, Boomer, Capone! C'mere! Time to go."

But the Labrabullies answered to no one. When they reached Baxter they started pacing around him, looking exactly like large animals do when they've found a good appetizer.

My phone started ringing in my pocket. I ignored it. "Baxter!"

The bully owner and I were at a fast trot toward the dogs now, the bullies closing their circle, their stalking faster.

But then Baxter dropped. Not like other dogs usually do at the sight of the bullies, trying to be invisible. Baxter went onto his back, showing his sweet belly and then writhed around as if to say, *It's okay, smell me.*

Which is exactly what the bullies did. No lunging, no more snarling. By the time the owner and I reached them, the three were cozied up to one another, the bullies nudging Baxy with their noses, as if they loved him, finally ready to play.

"Jesus Christ," the owner muttered, chuckling and looking down at the dogs. "I've never seen them like this." He looked at me. "You got a special dog."

"Thanks," I said, taking a breath of relief at the sight of Baxter batting a paw at one of the bullies who replied by simply ducking his nose, ready to take another punch.

"What's that collar he's got?" the guy said.

"I made that collar to piss off my ex-husband."

This caused him to laugh.

I told him about how Sebastian hated it and always tried to replace it with something plainer.

"He's crazy," the guy said. "That's a good-looking collar."

"Right?"

"Heck, yes."

I told him about the leash, how both had been in the video. He hadn't seen it, so I explained the video.

He pulled it up on his phone. He laughed and laughed, then played it a second time, actually holding it out for the bullies, who sorta seemed to watch it for a bit.

"You want me to make you one?" I said, immediately wondering if I'd taken the whole bully diplomacy a little too far.

But the guy just said, "Sure! Could you do one in red and another in blue?"

"You got it." We exchanged information. He took off the red collar of one of the bullies, and I eyeballed the size.

My phone started ringing again. I pulled it out of the pocket of my jeans. More surprise.

The screen read, *Mom.*

There is nothing more irritating than a person raised in a loving household, one who has been provided everything, but who finds something lacking in that setting. Nothing except being that person.

I knew this because I had always greatly disliked myself for feeling the lack of love from my parents, Simon and Muriel Champlin. They were so in love with each other that they were nearly oblivious to everyone else. It was clear how much they adored each other, and it was understandable. They were exceptional people who were exceptional together. And when two people love each other like they do, it's an exclusive thing. They tried to spread it to me. They tried. And they did love me in their way. But I always knew I didn't have what they did, that they couldn't feel toward me the way they did toward each other.

So my mother and I didn't speak with any regularity. But now she was talking quickly and excitedly. "I saw Baxter on TV!"

My parents lived out east, in a college town with a historical race course, and the only time they'd met Baxter was during a short holiday visit a year and a half ago.

"You saw it on TV or the internet?" I asked. My mother rarely watched TV.

"It just ran on our news here."

"Are you kidding?"

"No. I turned it on to see the weather. Your father is hoping to do some work outside tomorrow."

My parents were both artists. My father had been an urban planner first, then he became fascinated with remnants of demolished government and legal buildings. He eventually brought the materials home and retrofitted our garage to become his studio. He crafted large, avant-garde items—a huge witness stand from chunks of cement, a Doric column from cobbled shards of copper, the scales of justice from molded scrap metal. The town purchased the scales of justice to decorate the front of the courthouse.

Now such pieces were all my father did, and he got paid well for them.

My mother was a completely different artist. Technically trained and meticulously detailed, her oil paintings and mixed-media pieces were delicate, lovely. But there was also something savage within them—red streaks hidden deep in a meadow, a blade in a child's profile. My mother said she was exploring. My father, she said, had been the only person in her life to allow that exploration. It took her years, but finally a gallery in New York was interested in her. They represented her, helped create an audience for the double-edged quality of her art. She became a working artist. But she always catered to my dad, always put him first.

So now it made sense that my mother was watching the news only to check the weather for my dad, who lately took much of his work outside in decent weather.

I explained to my mother about the Baxter incident, how Vinnie shot the video and posted it, how it ran on Chicago's morning news. And now my mother was telling me it had been shown on her local newscast.

My mother asked me about the collar and leash, and I told her I'd sewn the stars on it, told her about the sale I'd just gotten from the Labrabullies' owner.

"Good for you! They're gorgeous!" My parents were happiest when I was being creative, the way they were. "We have neighbors who just got two Irish setter puppies. Would you make the same collars for them? We want to give them a gift."

"Sure, I'd love to." It was always a treat to feel a sense of cohesiveness with one of my parents (even if only about dog accoutrements).

"Honey," my mom said, her voice holding a little trepidation, then trailing off at the end. Finally she said, "I know this Baxter thing is fun, but is it okay? I mean are you okay?"

"I'm very okay, Mom. I'm actually great."

"Is any of this excitement about the video bringing up past…inclinations?"

I felt a flash of irritation. "Mom," I said in a low, strained voice. "I never had those inclinations. That's not why it happened."

Here was the other reason my parents and I didn't talk often. They knew about the Amalie Project and what had led to it.

"I know," my mother said. "You've told me that. But we worry."

"Don't!" I wanted to say, *Why didn't you worry about me when I was growing up? Why didn't you ever worry until I was in too deep? Before I slipped away?*

My mother sighed. "Okay, okay." Silence and then she asked, "So when do you think you can have the collars done for the puppies?"

"I'll put it at the top of my list." I wanted to be

nice to my mom. There was no reason not to be. She and my dad were who they were, never anything else. "I'll send them within a few days."

"Oh, take your time. Don't put stress on yourself."

"It's not stress."

"You just don't want to get so overwhelmed that you go back to past habits."

"Mom!"

"I'm sorry, I'm sorry."

I took a deep breath. I asked about my dad. She gave me a quick rundown—all was good—and then she was off to find her husband.

7

The next call surprised me even more than my mom's.

Sebastian.

He'd seen the video online, and he actually sounded a tad excited himself. Not like my mom had, but definitely amused, interested.

"Isn't it hysterical?" I told Sebastian about Baxter darting and Vinnie shooting the whole thing.

We fell right into conversation, the way we used to a long time ago—no awkward "Hi, how ya been feeling? Okay, how about you?" chitchat.

When something like this happened—rarely, I grant you—it made me remember that when we were "us," Sebastian and I had a hell of a lot of fun.

One of the reasons I'd shut down my online dating profile without even going on a date was because I feared that no one could be quite as fun as Sebastian when he wanted to be. And I knew fun, having been deeply involved (way too deep, it would turn out) in my teens and twenties with a touring rock band.

The problem, toward the end of us, was Sebastian hadn't desired much fun with me. It had made me terribly wistful—remembering the days when Sebastian was on, when we were engaged. Sometimes, he would wake me at five in the morning and he would make some crazy dish—whatever he'd found at the ready-market that morning, whatever his imagination lit upon. Once, it was pretzels and scrambled eggs with cheese and hot sauce. His were the most bizarre breakfasts and the most delicious because he infused them with that fun. He brought that sense of fun to each day. He loved to "call an audible," as he put it, hitting a last-minute Cubs game, or going to see a blues band at Kingston Mines.

But there was no such fun like that in the last year of our marriage. It was one of the factors that made me say, *Okay, let's give up*.

But the conversation about our child dog was fun. "And you know it was on the news," I told Sebastian.

"What do you mean?" He didn't sound so amused. "Who was on the news?"

"Baxter. On Pamela's morning show. It wasn't just a video on the internet."

He groaned.

"What?"

"They must have been desperate."

"It was cute," I said. "And then my mom called from New York. It was on their news, too."

"Are you kidding?"

I ignored the slightly scornful tone.

"My mom called," I repeated. I knew that would stop him. He knew I had issues with my parents that had been visited and revisited at therapists' offices.

"Oh?" he said.

"Yeah. We had a great conversation."

I told Sebastian about it. And maybe he was in a good mood—maybe because I'd mentioned my parents and he knew that could be a tough situation for me—because soon, he softened, I could tell. It was his tone when he responded, asked questions, it was the volume of his voice, too, that showed his level of interest. I was awarded with his full attention—questions illuminated with years of hearing about Simon and Muriel Champlin.

"How old are they now?" he said.

"Sixty-six. My mom's sixty-five."

"My mom's seventy next year." He told me of his own recent conversations with his mom. Not that his mom was anything like mine. On the contrary, she loved and adored Sebastian so much that I was pretty sure that she was secretly relieved at our divorce. That should have made me feel bitter, I suppose, but instead it only made me feel more wistful when I thought of the kind of mother's love and adoration he got from her.

Sebastian scoffed. "I can't believe the dog was on the news out in the sticks."

It was the scoff that brought me back. I had heard that scoff too many times.

"What's up, Hess?" I said, putting on a chummy tone. "You've got a problem with your dog being on a video?"

"Well, it's not news."

I wanted to bite back. But that would only start up an argument. I changed the topic, and we talked for a few minutes about nothing.

And as often happened when Sebastian and I had some kind of clash on the phone, or in this case a near clash, I took to walking around the condo, Baxter, our de facto kid, at my feet. We had spent time designing and decorating every room. The condo was our first real place together (he'd moved into mine when we were in New York). There was the joint office, and the master bedroom with the Moroccan-inspired leather headboard, the wide-planked hardwood floors we'd chosen for throughout the rest of the condo. We'd done it together. Hence, this condo was *ours*. I still felt like that most of the time.

But when we fought, and I walked the place, that's when I could remind myself that this was mine now.

It took some of the sting away from Sebastian's haughty opinions about what constituted *news*. I don't know if he ever understood how much it hurt when he did that, especially back when I was working for a local magazine he considered "just a soci-ety rag—it's a grown-up yearbook."

That reminder rankled me, and I asked how his trip was going, just to bug him.

I got a few mumbled words in response.

"C'mon, where are you?" I asked, not because I thought he'd tell me, but more because I wanted to needle him.

"Jess," was all he said in a tight voice.

I sighed.

I went into the kitchen with its 1950s dining chairs and the kitchen table, which had been Sebastian's grandfather's worktable, adorned with new legs.

"You're back when?" I said. Another jab.

But he didn't take the bait. "I do love you, Jess," Sebastian said.

I waited, then muttered, "I love you, too." Even though it didn't matter.

We were both silent.

"Sebastian," I said his name back to him. Not with a question mark, just said it.

At his name, Baxy seemed to have realized who I was talking with. He'd been playing with an old sock of Sebastian's, but then his head shot up and he ran over, jumped on a kitchen chair, black nose in the air, pink tongue hanging from his mouth in a happy pant.

We fell quiet again, and in the silence of me and

Sebastian, I leaned over and stroked Baxter's neck. He stretched his head up to allow more.

Then Sebastian had to go, and I said goodbye. I'm not sure he heard me.

When I hung up, Baxter looked at me, then looked around, his eyes quickly scanning the room, darting back to me. I could hear him thinking, *But where is he?*

"Gone," I said. "Gone."

8

Sebastian returned to Chicago a week after he left. A short trip for him. He called on the way home from the airport.

"How's Superdog?" he said when I answered.

I looked at Baxter, who sat on the checkerboard kitchen floor, patiently waiting for me to scoop his lunch into his bowl.

"He's super."

"I missed him."

"I know."

Baxter always seemed to ground Sebastian. When we'd first gotten him, Sebastian was suddenly happier working in the home office—the office we'd outfitted just to make Sebastian feel inspired, feel as if he was back in New York, with a row of state-of-the-art TVs that showed—close-up and raw—news stations around the world. The BBC usually ran on the monitor closest to him, except for Saturdays in the fall when all the TVs bore college football, the most prominent being whichever game Iowa was playing in.

Sebastian had gone to Iowa, strictly for the writing program. Creative writing. He didn't know then that he would stray to journalism, that it would hook him in and turn him on in a way that was different from creative writing. He suddenly knew one day in his senior year, in the middle of a seminar on fiction writers who turn to nonfiction. He didn't want to make people up. He wanted to write about the people who *were*. War reporters and investigative journalists—those were the heroes, those were the people he wanted to be. After graduating he spent years living in Italy, working on a book exposing various Berlusconi scandals.

I met him a year after his first book on Italian politics was published. It was such a lively book—written in a lively voice about admittedly lively people who had a lot of sex—that it was on the bestseller lists for two weeks, enough to get him another contract. It had made him sparkle, that book deal, which had just been inked the day we met. The sparkle gave him something beyond the sexy hair, the strong jaw, the soft eyes that didn't so much bore into yours as melt into them, and that bottom lip of his. It made him reverberate with charisma.

On the kitchen floor now, Baxter rolled over to show his belly. *Rub me, please!*

I bent and put my hand on his warm dog belly,

using him for comfort while I broke the news to Sebastian. I told him that since he was gone, Baxter's video was still running on news stations around the country, the web video getting nearly half a million hits.

"Christ," he said. "That's crazy."

I said nothing, waiting for a nice whip of sarcasm.

He waited, too, probably for me to make some crack about his attitude, launch into the ruts of priors.

Instead, Sebastian took an audible breath. "How is he handling it?" he asked.

I looked down at Baxter again, who flipped back to a sit. He thumped his tail, then tilted his head as if he expected something, a trait I couldn't recall him doing before. "He might be getting a bit of child star syndrome," I said. "Possibly impatient. But otherwise he's great."

I put Baxy's food on the floor and he gave my wrist a quick lick in thanks before he nose-dived into the bowl. "Nah," I said to Sebastian. "Not really. He's still our little guy."

"I miss him," he said again.

"I know," I said again.

We chatted for a few minutes about some clients who had recently retained me again to outfit them for a wedding, about the magazine editors I'd had lunch with last week who'd promised work, about a good friend of Sebastian's who had sold a book, about Sebastian's family.

It would be the last normal conversation we would have for a long time. If I had known it, I might have thought to couch what I told him next. "The national news is going to run it."

"What?" A distinctive snip to his voice that I knew meant displeasure.

"Baxter's video."

"What national news program?"

I wasn't sure. I told him a producer had called.

"What was his name?"

I looked at the stack of cut up, old index cards that I used for notes in the kitchen. I read off the person's name.

"Jesus, are you serious?" Sebastian said. "I know that guy. Does he know Baxter is my dog?"

"I don't think so. I didn't mention it because it didn't seem like you'd want people to know that."

He exhaled in a short burst, as if through clenched teeth. "I have to go." He hung up.

Yet an hour later, he was knocking at the door of my condo.

I peered through the keyhole and saw him. *This is* my *condo,* I thought. *Mine.*

Of course, Sebastian knew the doorman, who had simply let him up. Still, the building staff also knew we were divorced. It annoyed me that they would give him free reign, without so much as a warning call to me, even if it was to tell me he was elevator-bound.

I glanced down at what I was wearing—yoga clothes for a class I planned to attend—gray pants, a thin, hot-pink top. I reached back and pulled my hair over one shoulder, smoothing the front and tucking the other side behind my ear. It occurred to me only as I was in the middle of the action that I was doing it because that was how Sebastian liked it.

But he definitely wasn't in the mood to appreciate my hair.

He strode inside. "Hi." He stopped suddenly, as if realizing in that instant he didn't live there anymore.

"Hi?" I tried to keep the irritation from my voice, but it was hard.

"Where's Baxter?"

"He's playing at Daisy's house."

Sebastian looked a little blank.

"You know Daisy," I said. "From the dog park."

"I didn't know they had play dates," he said.

"Usually when one of us has to work. Maureen came and got him after we got off the phone."

Sebastian nodded. "Well, I just wanted to tell you, in person, that I got ahold of him."

"Who?"

"Paul." The national news producer. I opened my mouth, but Sebastian kept talking. "They're not going to run it."

9

After Sebastian spoke those words—*They're not going to run it*—I spun around and marched to our bedroom. I mean, *my* bedroom!

"Hey, Jess," I heard Sebastian say, still in the kitchen.

I kept walking, breathed in deep, then again and again. I had promised myself that I wouldn't let Sebastian make me sad or angry anymore.

I stepped into the bedroom and closed the door. I inhaled slowly. I was alive without him, I reminded myself.

After a minute I opened the door and, trying to tone down the marching, walked back to the kitchen. Sebastian sat on one of our kitchen chairs (*my* kitchen chairs), a leg crossed, ankle resting on the knee. He looked at me with a confused, maybe a little scared, expression. I couldn't read him like I used to.

"Why would you do that?" I asked.

"What?"

"Get the producer to cancel the piece on Baxter."

"Because it's not news."

"What do you care if your dog is on a news program?" I asked. "Even if it's not 'news'?"

"I happen to be a journalist who works in real news and I don't want anyone associating me with the dog video."

"Are you embarrassed by Baxter?"

"Of course not. Jesus."

"By me?"

A scoff.

"Well, then what? Do you think that some source in Pakistan won't give you information if he knows your dog is in a video?"

He said nothing.

"Will the army not let you embed with some troop?"

Sebastian scowled.

"Hey, just show them that he saved a kid." I shook my head. "Do you even care that the video makes people happy?"

"I'm not here to make people happy."

"Well, what if your ex-wife is expanding her business because of being on these programs? Would that make you even a little happy? What if *she* wanted to make people happy?"

"What do you mean?"

"I want to show you something." My breath was still short. I hadn't shown anyone, or even talked to anyone, about what I'd been up to this past week—staying up past midnight and getting up at five to work again.

I gestured at him to follow me. He stood. I walked him into the office.

Where Sebastian's desk used to be, a long folding table now resided. On the closest end was my sewing machine in front of a chair. In the middle was an empty space where I stood when I flipped through magazines, searching for inspiration, but rarely having to do so for very long.

I walked toward the far end of the folding table, Sebastian following me. There lay piles (organized by color) of plain, inexpensive dog collars and leashes, along with rolls of ribbon and small plastic boxes of embellishments.

I explained to Sebastian how people had been contacting me since the day of the video. "At first," I told him, "they wanted to order the Superdog collar or leash, sometimes both. It took me hardly any time to make them. Then things started expanding."

"Expanding how?" Sebastian stood with his hands behind his back, bent over my materials as if he were in a museum studying a display case.

I held up a few sheets of paper with print on them. "These are all the orders I have to fill in the next week."

Sebastian scanned the first page, then the next. "There are at least forty."

"I know. And I bet when I check my email, I'll have another five or ten."

He looked at me over the sheet. "Do you have a website?"

"Not for this. I have that static one for my styling business. People have been tracking me down through that. Like I said, first, they wanted the Superdog stuff. Now they're putting in their own ideas. It's like I take their idea, track down the materials and make it."

"Wow," Sebastian said. "That's amazing."

"Thanks. It's not technically that hard. The tough part is keeping track of everything and responding to everyone and then getting it shipped. But it's fun and creative, and now I'm starting to get all these ideas about designs for other dogwear and accessories."

"Dogwear?"

"I'm coining a new term. And no, I don't want your opinion on it."

He smiled, but barely. "Can I sit down?"

I waved my arm at the room and slightly shrugged like, *I can't stop you.*

Sebastian took the order sheet and sat on a light blue chair that had been his grandmother's. He'd never liked it, so I got to keep it. He didn't look at the order form, though. At first, his eyes roamed the office, maybe taking note of the loss of him in that room. The rest of his family's handed-down furniture was in his new apartment in Roscoe Village. Whenever I visited him there, I felt a little jealous, because the neighborhood was charming. There were wine shops and restaurants and boutiques of all kinds, and people strolled happily with their kids or their partners.

As Sebastian kept assessing the office, I wondered if he was noticing the things I'd added—like a painting of a ballerina I bought in New York when I was twenty-four and which Sebastian had found too feminine. It now hung in the spot that had once held Sebastian's framed map of Colonial America.

Suddenly, there was a crack of thunder, and a summer storm started pounding the windows, the room darkening. But strangely, neither of us moved. Sebastian's eyes kept sweeping the room, quickly taking stock the way he always did, taking mental notes. His eyes stopped when they reached mine, and again neither of us moved. An energy seemed to hold us there, one that felt both powerful and calm, no anger bubbling around the edges.

We were, I felt in that instant, observing a marriage that once was.

He uncrossed his leg and nodded at his lap.

A mix of surprise and longing arose within me. That nod was what Sebastian used to do when he wanted me to sit on his lap. Often the reason was to discuss something, other times it was because he wanted to kiss me. I didn't know which reason was applicable here. I hesitated.

"Jess," he said in a voice that was tired but caring.

I walked across the room and perched on his legs, a movement that felt so familiar it caused an ache. Sebastian felt warm. He smelled faintly of the fragrance he wore that was part leather, part something like lavender. That scent alone had made me swoon many a time. I leaned back a little.

"You know what this reminds me of?" he said. "Block Island."

I took a breath, emotions coursing through me. Block Island was where I first told him I loved him.

I had actually known that I loved him just a few months after meeting him, but I kept quiet. Turns out I didn't have to wait long. Just a few weeks after my realization, we were at a party and he stopped me when I came out of the bathroom, no one else in the hallway. "I love you, you know. So much."

I pretended to ruminate upon that revelation, said I needed to warm up to the idea of love. Technically, it was true. Because I knew—all too well—the destruction that could result from love.

But then one summer night, I returned the sentiment. We were lying in a rented room in Block Island—sandy sheets, candles in hurricane lamps—and I said it into his chest. "I love you, too."

He was so happy. He squeezed me hard. He kissed me on the top of my head, then pulled me up and kissed my forehead, then my eyes, then my mouth. We murmured the words to each other over and over.

Soon after, he fell asleep quickly, as if hearing those words from me had finally allowed him to relax. I watched as his sable brown eyelashes fluttered with dreams, and it hit me. *I will lose him.*

I understood, in that moment, or maybe I should say that I remembered, that all things end, especially good things. At some point, either Sebastian would die or I would or we would break up. At some point, I would lose him. That recognition cut sharply through me, so exquisitely painful.

Tears sprang from my eyes that night on Block Island. I choked on a quick-rising sob.

"What?" Sebastian said, waking fast. A confused look around, his journalist eyes taking in and registering the details of where, what, who and when.

His eyes had looked at me, those eyes the same chestnuty-sable color as his lashes. "What is it, baby?" he said.

I took a deep breath, let it fly. I explained what I was thinking, feeling, realizing, about the eventual end of us.

He pulled me tight to him again. He brushed my bangs off my forehead and kissed my temples, my eyes. "You won't lose me," he said.

I knew that Sebastian meant what he'd said. I also knew that, unintentionally, he'd been lying.

"Block Island was great," I said now, in my apartment. I stood up.

Block Island is over. And I am alive without you.

After a moment, Sebastian stood, too. He walked to the end of the folding table and fingered the various collars, leashes, embellishments.

He held up a pink string of flowers that would be placed on a white collar for a teacup poodle. "Promise me," he said, "that you won't put this on Baxy's collar."

"I promise."

"So you like doing this?" Sebastian gestured with his hand at the dog accoutrements across the table.

"I don't like it," I said.

He looked at me, raised his eyebrows.

"I love it."

Sebastian sighed. "I thought you were going to say that."

"Why the disappointment?"

He breathed out heavily—not as weary as his sigh, but close.

"Seriously, Sebastian, what's your problem with this?"

He shook his head.

"Really," I said, "what is it?"

"No problem," he said. He pulled his phone out of his pocket. "I'm going to call Paul, the producer, and I'm going to tell him to run the show."

10

Later I would think about how my showing Sebastian my dogwear business convinced him to call his friend the news producer. Therefore, I realized, I had essentially started my own demise—the outing of the past Jess behind the present one.

But it wasn't that first national news piece that did it. Destruction takes a little while.

The night Baxter was on the national news, a few days after the phone call, Sebastian dropped Baxter off because I needed him to try on dogwear.

"I'll get him tomorrow afternoon," Sebastian said.

"Sure. Thanks for doing this."

"Sure," he echoed.

Awkward silence seemed to course through the kitchen.

"So Baxter is on the news tonight." I figured he'd remember, but I wanted to see his reaction.

His face was neutral. "Yeah. I'm going to be at my mom's."

"Tell her hi."

Sebastian nodded.

I looked at my watch. "Damn, it's on soon."

He glanced at his phone then. "Shit." He sighed. "My mom has all her sisters coming over." Sebastian loved his four aunts, but they could be a lot to take when they were all together.

"That'll be fun," I said.

He groaned. "I'm so tired from writing all day. I just don't know if I can handle the coven." His mom had the maiden name of Carey, so the sisters called themselves Carey's Coven.

"You can watch it here," I said.

Pause. "Yeah?"

"Yeah."

And so Sebastian and I watched the news piece together at my place, the place that had once been ours.

The last time we'd shared an evening in the condo, or at least attempted to share, was the night we got divorced. Neither of us wanted to be alone, but we didn't want to be with anyone else, either. Our attorney had said it would be a simple matter. *You'll just step up to the bench and answer, "Yes."*

But the lawyer hadn't told us, or maybe he hadn't understood, how painful it was to hear a judge, in a bored tone, say, *The spouses' irreconcilable differences have caused an irretrievable breakdown of their marriage.*

From the corner of my eye I'd seen something

like a wince from Sebastian when the judge had said that. I'd looked over and saw he was squeezing his eyes shut. Sebastian, the man who didn't close his eyes to combat and war and gruesome situations, had clamped his eyes shut, as if to ward off tears or pain.

But the anguish had kept coming as the judge had intoned, *The court determines that efforts at reconciliation have failed*

I'd closed my eyes then, too, trying to stop the questions in my own voice streaming through my head—*Did I make the best effort possible? Could we put it back together? Did we fail? Did I fail?*

We'd both been shocked at how simple the proceedings ended up being, when nothing about our marriage had been simple.

But that night when Baxter was on the news, everything was just...lighter. Sebastian's latest article, a piece on militias in Libya, had just released, and the story garnered raves and much attention, making him relaxed, open. And I was certainly in a much better mood than the night we got divorced. And then there was our little boy—our Baxy on TV, bounding across a street and saving a little girl in a yellow dress.

Clara's mom was interviewed, holding Clara on her lap.

"Oh, watch this," I said, nudging Sebastian on the couch next to me. I lifted one of Baxter's paws and pointed it at the TV. "Watch, Baxy. They're talking about you."

As usual, Baxter registered little through the television.

The correspondent had arranged, toward the end of Clara's interview, for Baxter to surprise her and her mom. When the door opened and Baxter bounded through it to Clara, she shrieked happily and laughed with delight, wrapping her arms around Baxy. I couldn't imagine any viewer being unmoved. "Look at you, good dog!" Sebastian said, as Baxter bounced from my lap to his, panting with apparent delight at his parents sitting next to each other, happy.

"And hey, Jess, there you are," Sebastian said. He looked at me. "You didn't tell me they interviewed you."

"I wasn't sure you'd like it."

"As long as they don't ask to interview me."

He looked back at the TV, listening to the correspondent's voice-over. *Jessica Champlin, Baxter's owner, was surprised the star-studded collar she created for her dog would get such attention.*

Then my voice on TV saying, "I've gotten orders from around the country for the collars and leashes."

Sebastian held his hand up for me to high-five.

The news segment ended with a shot of Clara and Baxter, as she kissed his head. Then the screen flashed to that moment when Baxy tackled her, when the truck swerved around the corner.

"Well," the newscaster said. "That's something you don't see every day."

"Although we wish we did," his co-anchor said.

Sebastian patted my leg as the news rolled into a segment about taxes. I muted the TV and almost immediately a series of low *ding, ding, ding* sounds came from my phone. I picked it up.

"I have thirty-four new emails," I said. *Ding, ding, ding.* "And fifteen texts."

"Really?" Sebastian moved closer to me. "Since when?"

In my in-box, there was a bevy of emails with similar subject lines—Want to buy a Collar. How can I place order? Saw your dog on the news. Want Superdog collar. Need Superdog Leash.

"A few minutes ago."

Then it kept going – *ding, ding, ding.*

"There's more," I said, holding out the phone to show Sebastian. "A lot more."

11

It was Victory, the politician, who really kicked my business of dog styling into gear. She'd seen the news, too. She texted me the next morning, saying that she was being photographed that very afternoon for a women's magazine. Because the magazine hired a stylist, she hadn't needed to call me.

What's the angle of the article? I wrote.

The piece dealt with fashionable, powerful women in state government. They wanted to shoot her in her office.

But since I saw your dog on the news, she wrote, I'm thinking we need a shot w/me and dog.

Projects authority, I wrote.

Right.

If you can master dog, you can master the country.

Exactly!

But also shows warmth.

I need warmth! Victory wrote. We've pushed ball-buster image pretty far.

A few minutes went by, then Victory texted, The magazine loves the idea of the dog in the shoot! Calling you...

"You know, it's hard being a black politician," Victory said when I answered. She rarely made use of hellos, something I liked about her, and she nearly always said something random without explanation. "Do you think DeeDee needs a bath?" she asked.

"Everyone needs a blow out," I said. "When was the last time she was groomed?"

"Two months."

"Then for a photo shoot? It's time."

"Any chance I can hire you to style her?" Victory asked.

I thought about the work in the office, much of it buried under boxes of materials that had arrived just an hour before. Still, this was exactly the kind of thing I wanted to stay open to. It was, I realized, the exact kind of work I wanted to expand into. Dog styling—probably not much work out there but even less competition.

"Absolutely," I said to Victory. "I'll find a grooming appointment. And I'll pick her up."

"God love you. And however you want her fur to look is good for me," Victory said. "I'll pay you your usual."

"Sounds good," I said. "What is Dee wearing?"

"Wearing? Like her collar? It's the same one you saw last year."

"The olive green one?"

"Yeah. It's cute, right?"

"I think you want her to show a little sass."

"Good point," Victory said. "What's your thought?"

I'd been sitting at the kitchen table, but I stood and headed for the office. "Do you see her in a baby-pink?"

"No," Victory said. "I can't look like a socialite with a purse dog."

"One that's already called DeeDee."

"Precisely," she said.

"Got it." I picked up a few more things. "I'll have options."

We hung up, and I lifted a purple canvas strap with lime-green trim.

By the time I got to the photo shoot that afternoon, I'd made a few other collars and harnesses. As they were styling Victory's office, I showed her the various collars I'd made or brought.

Melody, Victory's thirteen-year-old, came home from school and helped us narrow the collars down further to the preppy purple-and-green one and a playful lavender one with white suns. We put both of them on DeeDee.

"Notice what you're wearing?" I pointed to Victory's own wrist, where she wore a watch and a bracelet. "The two at once?"

Victory looked down. "They look good together."

"Right," I said. "So do hers. Let's leave her in both collars."

"Yeah!" Victory's daughter said, and snapped a photo. "I'm posting this."

"You know she has more followers than I do?" Victory said as we walked DeeDee to the set.

"Your daughter? How is that possible?"

"She's in this youth choir that has played all over the country. She drives traffic to *me*."

The photographer liked the two collars, liked the texture and color it leant the photo.

Victory's daughter took another picture during the photo shoot.

My dog, Dee Dee, is so cool, the Tweet said. She's Superdog #2, then just #Superdog.

That photo and the comments were reTweeted by Melody's friends and Victory and her followers, and then the hashtag *Superdog* started getting repeated, which just fueled the story. Pet owners raced to post a pic of their own pup so they could claim to be something like *Superdog #87*. Or *Superdog #114*. Always they ended it simply #Superdog. Quickly the race ramped up and people were bragging that their dog was in the top thousand, then the top ten thousand. Soon, #*Superdog* was trending again.

It multiplied and multiplied. And multiplied. And, at least for a while, I felt very, very alive.

12

"You really don't have a great throw," I heard.

Baxter and I were at the dog park a few days after Victory's photo shoot, and I was using a Chuckit! stick to throw his green ball. We hadn't been out there enough lately, and in trying to fill all my orders, we kept missing our usual crew of dogs and owners.

Today, as always, Baxter had tore into the park as soon as I'd unhooked his leash. But when he didn't see his dog friends, he'd raced back to me, plunked the ball at my feet and had taken off again, looking over his shoulder as he'd run. I could almost hear him saying, *Go long, go long*.

But now someone else's voice. "You really don't have a great throw."

I turned to see a guy laughing. He wore a pink button-down shirt, cuffed at the arms with shorts and brown loafers. "Former prepster gone casual"—

the loafers weren't fussy, the guy's blond hair was a little shaggy.

I looked at Baxter, who stood panting at the base of a tree, his eyes trained upward to the branches where the ball had traveled.

"Yeah," I said, pointing to the throwing stick, "and I can't even blame it on anything."

The guy took a few steps, shook the branches of the tree, and the ball fell to the grass.

"I take it you're not into softball." The guy threw the ball for Baxter, sending him streaking across the grass.

"Nope," I said. "I'm into other things. Like jiu-jitsu."

Sebastian had taken years of jiu-jitsu classes, mostly with former college wrestlers who wanted to continue hand-to-hand fighting with the martial art, a skill Sebastian very much wanted to learn.

I had no idea why I had blurted that out, except that I thought it would be funny. I was becoming more and more bold. The latest social media wave about Superdog just made me more so. I was loving the attention and so was my business. I'd received calls and emails from over ten countries, and the orders for the collars and leashes increased, along with requests to style dogs (or people with their dogs).

The guy's brown eyes widened a bit, apparently impressed. I liked the combination of a blond with brown eyes.

"Do you know jiu-jitz?" I asked. "Jiu-jitz" was what the devotees called it.

"Sure, I know it." He was definitely impressed.

"I trained with the Gracies." The Gracies were Brazilian brothers with whom Sebastian had trained.

"Wow. Seriously?"

"No," I said, finally.

We both laughed.

Baxter ran back to the guy and dropped the ball at his feet.

"Smart dog," he said.

The guy threw the ball far across the park, and we watched Baxter retrieve it. When he brought it back, he sat at the man's feet for a minute, panting.

A college-aged guy walked along the sidewalk near us, a friend of his trailing behind, immersed in his phone. "That looks like Superdog," he said.

"It is Superdog," I said.

"Shut up!" The guy turned and called over his shoulder. "Frank, check this out! It's Superdog."

The two of them began petting Baxter, who obliged by licking their ears and eventually turned over and allowed his belly to be scratched.

The blond man was still standing there. "I heard about that Superdog video," he said.

I told him briefly about my experience of it. "It's been a weird ride," I said.

"That's cool," the blond said. He reached his hand out. "Gavin."

I shook it. "Jessica." I nodded at Baxter who was reveling in the attention from the college kids. "His real name is Baxter."

"Baxter," Gavin repeated. "Good name. How did you pick it?"

"My ex worked with someone with the name Baxter, and I liked it."

I didn't tell him that at the time we named Baxter, I was also hoping that by agreeing to the name I would soon meet Bill Baxter, the photographer Sebastian had long traveled with.

When Baxter came into our lives, the puppy gave us steam, rolled Sebastian and I through another year together, allowed my anger about not being let into his life simmer, allowed him to believe for a while that we could go on like that and I wouldn't need to ask about his job again. But steam dissipates—it fades. What remained was my disappointment, his inability to share. We were both sad. We had both reached the limits of being patient with a life that wasn't what we had hoped for or to the standards we set for ourselves.

But when Sebastian assumed he would get custody of Baxter, I was entirely alone in my emotions— shock and hurt. Admittedly, it had been Sebastian who had introduced the idea of a dog, a project we could share together, while I merely went with his desire because I wanted to give us another shot. But did that mean he got the dog?

I remembered the night vividly. We were at dinner again, picking over details of our divorce. The restaurant, Kamehachi, was in Old Town, usually a scenic stroll from our Gold Coast condo in any season. But it had dumped rain that Friday night, giving the streets an eerie-dark, postmodern look.

We'd been frequenting our favorite Chicago restaurants—Girl & the Goat, RL, Hugo's Frog Bar, Telegraph. We knew we were breaking up, but it was as if we were still debating the pros and cons, and I guess we thought the happy places where we'd eaten in the past would either (a) deliver some of that old magic and turn us around, or (b) at least make breaking up a tiny bit pleasant, therefore making us both agreeable.

By that night, it seemed we knew that we were 99 percent done. Still, we fell into an argument (rewind Volume II, *The Fights of Sebastian and Jess*). After that, we went silent for a long time, save for the soft clacking of enamel chopsticks. We dunked dumplings in thin broth, swirled green wasabi into soy.

And then, in really amicable tones, we somehow started negotiating the bulk of our split.

"I would want you to have most of the furnishings," Sebastian said. "Because you'll keep the condo."

I appreciated the offer as much as the assumption that I would stay in the condo. Sebastian, as a native of Chicago, could stay with his mother or a host of buddies before buying or renting a place in one of the many neighborhoods he already knew.

"You should take all the kitchen gear," I said.

When we got married, we didn't register for much, but those things we did sign up for—the pasta maker, the food processor, the knife sharpener—those were all for Sebastian.

So went that night. Trying to act like it was all oh so normal, we went back and forth—*you take that, I'll take this*. To smooth the discussion, we ordered a bottle of sake. And somewhere, somehow, we found a little ease (although ease itself was tough because it inevitably led my mind back to the possibility that we should stay together, ignoring all the things that wouldn't, or couldn't change).

"Hey," Sebastian said at one point, tipping a little more sake into my glass, "I'll be a real gentleman, and I'll give you the llama." We laughed. The llama had been a gift from a source for a story Sebastian had met in Chile. Made of colored straw, the thing was odd, over a foot tall. Sebastian had become close to this source, who'd been injured while attempting to get Sebastian information, and so he couldn't bear to throw it away. But where to put it? We'd tried the bathroom, but it loomed over the sink, as if about to drink from a small pond. Neither of us could handle it in the bedroom where its red straw took on an evil glint in low light. Eventually the thing migrated to a corner of the small den off the bedroom where, sometimes, Baxter liked to knock the llama onto its side and take naps with it.

"I don't want that llama!" I'd said. More laughing, more sake. I picked up a dragon roll, thinking, *It could be like this. It doesn't have to be all bad, all pain.*

"Fine, fine," Sebastian said. He gave an exaggerated sigh, as if caving in on some big point. "Since I'm keeping Baxy, and he's the only one who likes the llama, I'll take it off your hands."

I plunked my chopsticks on the table. Unfortunately, I'd just placed a large roll in my mouth. *Could they not make these things smaller or cut them in half?* I held my hand over my mouth and chewed as fast as possible, all the while trying to prevent eel and avocado from falling on my chin. By the time I was done, Sebastian was onto another topic, in mid-speech about our joint office and how, of course, he'd take his desk and I, mine. "And that chair in the bedroom," he was saying, "it was Mom's originally, so I'll grab that. The rest is yours."

Sebastian had a pinkish glow on his high cheekbones, above the barely there, dark stubble that lately was a permanent fixture on his face. The glow, I knew, meant a slight buzz and, definitely, happiness. But I wasn't sharing the emotion.

"You are *not* keeping Baxter!" I said. Loud.

Sebastian blinked as if he was a little surprised.

"Baxter is *my* dog, too!" I said. The thought of

no Baxter in my life, along with no Sebastian, drew tears.

"Hey," Sebastian said. He scooted his chair to mine, awkwardly patting my blond hair. We no longer knew how to touch each other.

"I know you love Baxter," Sebastian said.

I pulled my head away from his touch. "I do. I love Baxter!" My voice was cracked at the end. A woman on the other side of Sebastian glanced at me sympathetically.

I paused, and then like a bride at a wedding, I repeated the words, intoning, "I do."

Sebastian picked up on the wedding lingo. "Then, by the power vested in me by the State of Illinois and the Great Fatherhood of Dogs, I grant you, Jessica…" he paused "…joint custody of Baxter."

It was the last time I remember feeling married to Sebastian.

Now, in the dog park, I heard the college students saying goodbye to Baxter, and I pulled myself away from thoughts of that night.

When they left, Gavin threw the ball for Baxter again. And I wrenched myself back to the present. Enough of reviewing Sebastian and Jess, I told myself. Enough.

So when Gavin said, "I know this is kind of quick, but would you want to have a drink sometime?"

I said, "Sure." No hesitation.

Gavin looked at me, smiled. His teeth were white

against the light tan of his skin, his brown eyes crinkled. "How about today? There's a bar up the street that allows dogs."

He knew this, he told me as he threw the ball for Bax, because he used to have a red Labrador retriever named Wrigley. Sometimes, like today, he walked the same path he and Wrigley had when he was alive. Often, he and Wrigley had a beer after.

"Or I had a beer," he said. "Wrig was happy at my feet."

"Do you miss him?"

"Yeah."

"I understand a little," I said. "I have joint custody of this one." I pointed to Baxter.

"Really? Or is this like the jiu-jitz?"

"No, this is real. My ex-husband and I got him when we were together. We got divorced. So now we split him. Sounds screwed up, I know."

And right then, as if in silent agreement, Gavin and I and Baxter began walking to the bar. He asked more about the video and I told him about all the media Baxter had gotten.

"He seems to be doing well enough," Gavin said. He pointed to Bax who trotted just ahead of us, pulling a bit on the leash, as if he was looking forward to a beer.

Gavin held the door open when we reached the place, which was dim, edged with sunlit windows. We took a seat at the bar and fell into an easy conversation about dogs. Baxter settled in on the floor, and the bartender brought him a bowl of water.

Gavin told me about Wrigley, who he had gotten from a rescue while in college and who had lived to the age of seventeen.

"Where did you get this one?" Gavin asked, pointing to Baxter.

I told him about the farm in the middle of Amish country in Indiana where my ex and I had gotten Baxter.

And I found something interesting—namely, I felt comfortable, suddenly, talking about Sebastian in the past tense. I wasn't always saying the word *husband* then amending, "I mean, my *ex-husband*." It just came out "my ex" and I kept talking. And the more time I spent right there, in that moment, the more I had a hard time pulling myself away from Gavin's smile, his eyes. I wondered if he was as special as he seemed, as he looked, if we were as connected as it suddenly felt we were.

He mentioned something about his job, and I asked what it was.

"I'm in magazines." He paused. "What?" he said. "What's that look on your face?"

I laughed. "You're a writer." As easy as my ex had been to discuss, I wanted to date someone different from Sebastian.

Gavin held up a palm. "No, no. I'm not a writer.

Really." He peered at me. "But wait a minute—what's wrong with writers?"

"My ex," I said. "He's a writer."

"Ah. What kind of writing? Or shouldn't I ask?"

"No, it's okay." I let the thought of Sebastian run through my head, and found that again, for the moment, it didn't bring about a wave of sadness or regret. "Investigative journalism."

"What kind of investigations?"

"War correspondent. International human rights. That kind of thing."

"'That' kind of thing?" Gavin hung his head. When he raised it, he wore a sheepish grin. "He's just one of those selfless guys who wants to right wrongs and makes sure our overseas heroes don't go unsung."

"Or he's one of those rush junkies."

"Is he?"

"At least a little." I shrugged with one shoulder. "So what do you do in magazines?"

"I sell ad space."

"You don't sound happy about it."

"I'm a little disenchanted right now." But he sounded good-natured. He smiled, and that smile was easy. There was something there that was familiar, some look that was both pleased and delighted and… Ah, suddenly I remembered it. His look, which left my eyes briefly to sweep around my hair, my lips, before zooming back to me. That look I'd once seen from Sebastian a long time ago.

It was a look of excitement for the future. For potential.

13

The morning after I met Gavin I was lying in my bed when I got a text from Sebastian. But it was difficult to drag my attention away from the texts Gavin and I had been sending. They started with Nice to meet you, and Nice to meet you, too! and ran to the slightly flirtier, shaded messages we were exchanging now.

But finally I looked at Sebastian's.

You're in the news today, he wrote.

Hmmmm? I wrote back.

You're in the Trib.

I stared at that sentence. I couldn't tell if he was annoyed or okay with it.

I called Sebastian. "Morning."

"Hey."

"So, what does the article say?"

"Haven't seen it yet. One of the editors just texted me. I was just going to look it up."

"Don't worry about it," I said. I didn't want to deal with his hang-up about Superdog not being news. "Baxy and I will go out and get the paper."

By reflex, I reached toward the headboard where Baxter always slept.

"Oh, geez," I said, a little wave of sadness cresting over me. "I forgot he was at your place."

"He misses you," Sebastian said kindly.

And I missed Baxter then, like a fat fist to the gut.

I shook my head to shake out the thoughts. Baxter seemed as happy about being with Sebastian as he was with me, and that was what mattered.

"Thanks, Sebastian," I said. "Give Baxy a kiss. I'll talk to you later."

I would, I decided, get outside, even though I didn't have the dog, before I'd come back and get a solid workday in on my dogwear. Lately, the days were getting hotter, the heat failing to leak out of the city much. First thing in the morning was the only relative cool Chicagoans were getting.

I took the elevator to the ground floor and went out the Goethe Street exit. A calm, powder blue sky lay comfortably over the world, while a yellow sun cast its heat behind me, rising higher over the lake.

I went to the pharmacy on the corner of State and Division, bought a few copies of the paper (maybe my parents would want one?) and quickly left.

"Baxy," I said under my breath as I walked back. "You're in the newspaper!" I imagined him in front of me, giving a little leap.

At the corner, a wrought iron bench was on the front lawn of an apartment complex. No one was around, so I dropped the papers on the bench and, still standing, flipped through one.

I found the article in the local celeb section of the paper. The photo had been lifted from the video and showed me holding Baxter. It was cute—Baxy with his tongue hanging out, looking as though he was grinning and laughing. It was a short piece about the trending video and the attention it had garnered, even in other countries.

I smiled. But then I caught the article next to it.

The headline read, McGowan Lands Another Award.

I closed my eyes and breathed in, promising myself that the breaths would help my nerves. Then I opened my eyes and let myself look at the photo.

There was Billy McGowan. There was my past.

Hurt and shame flamed inside me. And I couldn't believe how much it felt the same as it had back then. Such feelings could disappear but when they returned, they did so in force.

"Can I help you?"

I opened my eyes. A doorman in a brown suit and maroon tie stood in front of me. His eyes were pulled together in concern.

"I'm fine," I said. "Just reading…" I nodded at the newspaper, seeing the other two I'd put down were being blown by a hot breeze, their pages spreading open so that they now covered most of the bench.

"I'm sorry, ma'am. Our lawn is just for residents."

"Of course." I closed the paper, scrambled to pick up the others. And it all came floating back.

No one thought that Billy McGowan would be the star, a musical deity of sorts, who not only had talent that grew every time he played, but someone who lit up everyone else—his brothers in the band with him, the touring group of musicians, all the fans (boys and girls alike). And me.

When I first met Billy we were both just kids, newly teenaged, from a town where they raced horses in the summer and then largely slumbered during the winter.

Billy was the youngest of the three brothers, the one, initially, who was simply along for the ride. Mick, his oldest brother, was the one everyone adored back then. Smolderingly sexy Mick, with the deep black eyes and soulful lyrics that made every girl think, *I wish someone felt that way about me.*

Kevin, the second, was lovable and charming. He talked to everyone young and old, wanted to know about everyone. When my mother met Kevin after Billy and I started dating, she said, "He is as sweet as pie." Although I was envious of the smitten way my mother gazed at Kevin for that moment, a way she'd never gazed at me, and although I thought the phrase "as sweet as pie" was really stupid, I had to agree with her.

The early success of their band and the attention paid to Kevin and Mick (older than Billy by five and seven years respectively) was our heyday. Because it meant Billy was mine. Just mine. And I was his. As time went on, that became more and more clear.

"Je t'adore," Billy started saying to me. He was taking French while I had been postponing the required language classes to the end of high school.

"What does that mean?" I said.

He smiled, looking shy. But I knew him well at that point; I knew it was more a pleased expression than bashful. "It means I adore you," he said.

That word— *adore*—was one I had always wanted to hear in connection with myself. No, that wasn't quite right. Rather it was that phrase—*I adore you*— with emphasis on the *you* that I had always craved.

When Billy and I officially exchanged "I love yous" four months after we met, we said it at the same time. Our eyes were locked as they often were, but that look carried something even greater. "I love you," we said again at the same time.

Later, when I saw those music fans (I hated the term *groupies*) who stared with parted mouths at Mick, I felt camaraderie. The girls, the fans, they wished someone would feel the way about them that Mick sang about in his lyrics.

I knew exactly how they felt because not only did someone feel that about me, but I felt the same way about him.

So to lose that…and in the way that I did… Well, it was a terrible loss.

I jolted back to the present when I got inside my condo, but I still felt shaken by memories. Synapses inside my brain had connected to a place and time I'd thought I'd outrun, outpaced, outdone.

It was such a painful reminder of how my life (everyone's life, really) had the potential to be dismantled. Even if one had gone through a deep dismantling like I had, it could happen again, it could unravel further.

Fear took me over—fear of losing the life I'd cobbled together, the one that I was starting to come alive in.

But I couldn't shake it. A deep sense of foreboding crawled inside me, and it couldn't be discharged by breathing or perspective or distraction. It only grew that fear.

Finally, I turned off my phone, silencing the faint red light indicating new messages. Not even the potential of texts from Gavin could cheer me.

I turned off my laptop.

Then I got back in bed. And stayed there.

14

That day, I was in and out of a weird fog of a sleep, suddenly bone-exhausted.

I missed Baxter so much. I pined for that dog. Suddenly, it seemed silly that I'd agreed to *share* the dog with my ex-husband. It was too hard. I thought of how many people I knew who shared custody of children. My heart hurt thinking how hard it must be, how much they must miss their kids.

I sank further and further into a blue mood that seemingly wouldn't lift.

Until one moment. In that one moment, the bleakness I felt somehow led me to a recognition—I could decide not to give in to the fear. It was my choice.

Life wasn't always easy. I knew that. And the past could be full of mistakes and pain. Sometimes memories of that could hurt a lot, scare a lot. But it was still my choice as to whether to let fear be the only emotion that resided in me. I could be fearful,

I saw then, but still hopeful. I could be fearful and still move through life.

I sat upright. I got out of bed and looked at the clock. *Three o'clock*. I couldn't remember having stayed in bed that late since…

Again, for a moment, the memories. Back then, three-in-the-afternoon wake-ups were a way of life.

I shook away the thoughts. *I can be fearful and still move through life.*

I looked at myself in the mirror. I tried to pull back from my form and gain some perspective.

I looked at the whole of myself. Rather than my usual quick perusal—of my blond hair, my clothes, checking my hazel eyes to ensure no mascara had smeared, checking that pink lipstick did not dot my teeth—I took in all of me. At once.

Then I pulled on shorts and a T-shirt, determined to take a run.

I could choose new things. I could continue to change, to evolve if I really wanted to. Even if negative emotions ran through me, I could choose to stay open to things, even those things that scared me.

I ran a brush through my hair and pulled it back, keeping an eye on myself.

Maybe, I thought, I would sleep until three every day. Or maybe I would start going to clubs, to museums, to sailboat races, to horse races, to more street fairs, to see more music, to see the ballet. Maybe I would start cooking rather than carrying out. (Maybe

I would actually get one of the slow cookers people were strangely enthusiastic about.) Maybe I would develop a taste for green chilies. Maybe I would start going to church again. Maybe I would move to another city. Maybe to Paris. Or Santa Fe. Maybe I would learn a musical instrument.

That stopped me for a minute. I flashed again on the picture of Billy McGowan in the paper.

But I chose to discard that thought. And when I did, I had an idea. I suddenly knew what I wanted to call my business.

I grabbed a pad of paper off my nightstand and I wrote, "I'd Rather Sleep with the Dog."

Then I added, "a Jessica Champlin company."

I put the cap back on the pen.

Right when I was about to walk out the door, the phone rang.

"Hello?"

"Hey, Jessica?"

"Yes?" I didn't recognize the friendly voice.

"It's Toni Dalloway. I'm Victory's publicist."

"Hi, how are you?" I sat down on the bench next to the front door and pulled on my running shoes. I'd met Toni when she'd hired me to style Victory on a few occasions. "Thanks so much for styling DeeDee," she said. "I never would have thought to do anything special for the dog."

"Have you seen the images yet?"

"Yes, a bunch. And I love them. I'll send you a few. Hey, do you want to do more pet gigs?"

"Uh, well, I don't know. My line of dogwear is really heating up." I told her the name of my company.

"Are you serious?" she said. "I love that!"

Fueled by her enthusiasm, I asked her what she meant by "pet gigs."

"Well, all of a sudden, we're seeing more dogs being photographed with some of my clients. I mean, only if they actually own one, but it seems like such an interesting way to show part of someone's life."

I thought about it. I'd been hired to style a CEO at his office next week for *Crain's Chicago Business,* but I was leery of doing the typical "man of power at his desk with the skyline behind him" kind of thing. If the guy owned a dog, having the pup in the photo would totally soften him, something the company wanted since he had a reputation of being a shark.

But then I thought of how overwhelmed I'd be if I took on more work. And I chose not to take it. "Toni," I said, "I do want more work like this, but I'm just so swamped right now. Keep me posted the next time you need something."

"Well, there is one thing. And it's a bit time-sensitive so I have to tell you now. The mayor wants a photo op with Superdog."

I stood. "You're kidding. The mayor of Chicago?"

"Yep. Wish I could say I thought of it. But they called me."

I laughed. That was something I liked about Chicagoans on the whole—they were hardworking people who weren't afraid to give others credit for a good job or idea.

"The call came to me from his people who knew I worked with Victory. They saw her kid's picture with Victory and Baxter from the day of the shoot. Now the mayor wants his whole family to be in a picture with Superdog. They're going to consider sending it out as their holiday card."

"Wow," I said. Not only was this a great coup, but it was important for me on a deeper level—the mayor was tied to a huge decision I'd made after Sebastian and I first broke up.

"You want to do it?" Toni said.

"Hell, yeah," I said. And then I texted Gavin.

15

The mayor was a squat man with powerful shoulders and a head whose size appeared as if it was made for a larger person.

"Superdog!" He crouched, and Baxter ran to him as if he'd known him forever. Then he put his paws on the mayor's shoulders and began licking his ears.

"Baxy!" I said. "Don't."

"Oh, it's no problem," the mayor said. In one swoop, he picked Baxter up and tucked him under his arm like a football, then walked toward me, the other arm outstretched. Baxter panted happily. Maybe he sensed the power of the guy.

We were in the headquarters of what had once been Mayor Michael Flaherty's campaign office and was now a PR satellite office.

I was in a great mood because after getting off the phone with Toni yesterday and going for a run, I had spent much of the afternoon texting with Gavin. The texts had gone from those initial ones—Nice to meet you, Nice to meet you, too! to I want to kiss you from Gavin and me responding, Tell me when. His final text had been, Tomorrow night. Can't wait.

"You're Jessica," the mayor said when he reached me.

I shook his hand. "Yes, nice to meet you, Mr. Mayor."

"Please, call me Mike."

I almost said, *Really? Excellent!* Because Mayor Flaherty— Mike—had an unbelievable amount of charisma and deep blue eyes that looked right into you, but also, his very existence held some significance for me. The last election was the first time I voted in Chicago. Debating the mayoral candidates was something Sebastian and I had done when we needed a break from talking about us (and the demise of us). Sebastian loved using his journalistic skills to teach me about the candidates, the issues (oh, there were many in Chicago), and simply about the city itself and how unique it was.

The election rolled around on the same week Sebastian and I decided, officially, we could no longer survive. So deciding to vote in the mayoral race signaled for me another decision—I would stay in Chicago. I wouldn't return to Manhattan. There was nothing there for me, nothing at all. I'd only lived there originally because of Billy. And the more I thought about it, the more heartbroken I became at the thought of leaving Chicago. I hadn't realized I was truly in love with the city until Sebastian and I broke up. And at first I thought I was just staying in town because of our shared custody agreement with Baxter. But even though I was often sad when Baxter wasn't around (constantly imagining the tiny *clang-clang* of his dog tags) there was no other place, no other city where I wanted to be.

Like Billy, Manhattan had been a first love for me—intense, gripping, giving me no choice but to respond. But I liked the pace of Chicago. I liked the Midwest friendliness. I liked the creative edge that permeated everything.

"Okay…Mike," I said to the mayor. I stalled for a second on what to say next, whether I should gush. Then I realized my dog had essentially done that for me. I pointed to Baxter. "Sorry about the enthusiastic greeting."

"Hell, I wish I could get that kind of greeting from my kids. Or some of the aldermen."

Toni rushed in then, a whirl of black hair flying behind her and dressed in a black suit, black pumps. "Mr. Mayor," she said, rushing toward us.

"Mike, please."

She pumped his hand. "Good to see you again." She gave me a quick hug. "Good to see you, too, Jess!" She turned back to the mayor. "It looks like you and Superdog are getting along."

"Hell, yeah. I grew up with dogs. Retrievers."

I knew from reading about him that Mike Flaherty was from an old Irish family in Chicago. He'd also been an Olympic boxer before running a number of campaigns for other people. It was oft said that Flaherty embodied the old Irish ways—he put up a good fight, but he always believed in sharing a pint after.

Some of the mayor's aides materialized and introduced themselves. One started patting the mayor's nose with powder, which Mike seemed to barely notice.

"You're sure you're all right doing this?" he said to me, gesturing at a set on the other side of the office. It appeared permanent—a skirted area in red with a backdrop featuring tiny flags of Chicago. A draped pedestal had been placed in the middle of the set next to a tall stool.

"Of course."

"Great, great!" he said. "Why don't you sit here." He led us to the set and patted the stool, looking at me.

"Oh, I don't need to be in the picture," I said. "This is for you and Baxter."

"Just for me and Baxter?" He bounced the dog on his hip as if he were a child.

Baxter responded by gazing at him, his black mouth grinning and panting more. I'd once read in a dog behavioral book that panting when not exerted was a sign of happiness, almost of laughter.

"Hell, no! We want you in the photo," Mike said,

answering his own question. "My wife and kids and I—we've seen the video about eight hundred times. We love you guys!"

I shrugged. "Fantastic."

There was a time I would have modestly protested. But it sounded like fun. I thought what a good story this would make on my date with Gavin that night.

One of the staff members called to the mayor from across the room. A door opened then and in walked two blond boys in school uniforms and a woman with a blond bob.

The mayor introduced his wife, Deb Walker, who was taller than him and had a lovely smile. She gave me a warm handshake. She pointed at her kids. "And this is Charlie and Tate."

The mayor had put the dog on the floor and the boys were petting him. They waved.

"They're usually good about shaking hands," Deb said. "But they're too excited about Superdog, I think."

More staff members floated around us, as did a photographer and assistants, but progress on setting up the shoot kept getting waylaid by people's desire to say hi to Superdog. The Flahertys were remarkable in their ability to chat good-naturedly when we were all finally herded into the set area. More chairs were brought in, then the place was relit. All the while, the kids and various assistants played with Baxter, lifting him up on the pedestal.

When the photographer pointed at the stool for me to sit, I hopped up on it and adjusted the loose white cotton blouse I'd worn (fit for the tropical heat Chicago was now muscling through).

On the pedestal, Baxter obediently sat and stayed. He was wearing a new design of mine—two collars that fitted together, one on top of the other. A buyer could pick blue and orange for a Bears game on Sunday, then change it the next day to blue and red for a Cubs game. The one Baxter wore now was maroon on one side, gold on the other. I kept looking at Bax, fearing he'd leap off the pedestal, but the Flaherty boys were feeding him treats and holding on to him.

"This is fantastic!" Toni said from the edge of the set where she stood.

The photographer was evidently accustomed to fast shoots because despite sending in his assistants to adjust hair and clothing a few times, he got off a number of shots in fifteen minutes.

The mayor left in a flurry of people, waving over his shoulder. His wife and kids took a few more minutes and then the mayor's staff expertly hustled everyone out.

Toni, Baxter and I walked out onto LaSalle Street, right near the Dubuffet sculpture—a hulking black-and-white thing in the middle of a slick metro area. It felt as if we were at the hub of the city right then.

"That was amazing!" Toni said. She bent down and picked up Baxter, kissing him on the top of his golden head and putting him down.

"Thanks for getting us in," I said.

"Are you kidding?" She yanked off her suit jacket, threw it over her arm and pulled out her phone.

We found a sidewalk café and Toni went inside to get us iced teas. I sat in the shade of an L train rumbling occasionally overhead, thinking how fun the photo shoot had been, how…joyous. And all because I hadn't refused the mayor's offer to be in it. I had stayed open. I had let it be.

When Toni got back we sipped our tea and she told me how happy the photographer had been, and how much the mayor seemed to enjoy himself (which apparently wasn't always the case).

Her phone dinged. She looked down and read a few things. Her eyes went wide. "They're running it tomorrow in the paper."

"What?"

She held out her phone, showing me a message from the mayor's assistant. Then she put her phone back in her pocket.

I watched an L train snake by overhead, then I turned back to Toni. "I've got a business proposition for you."

"Tell me," she said.

"I wondered if you wanted to work with me."

Toni wore tortoiseshell sunglasses that curled up

at the edges of the frames, each dotted with a little crystal. She took them off and looked at me. "I am definitely listening."

"Well, here's the thing," I said. "My dog businesses are bringing in money, but I've got a lot going out the door to web development and supplies and shipping."

I told her how I couldn't keep up with the myriad of media requests. Although there were a few haters, many of the requests were very nice. We'd had two emails from the families of sick kids, kids who likely wouldn't be around in a year. One of their last wishes was to meet Superdog. Baxter and I were already making plans to fulfill those wishes. Then there were the ones from local papers or TV shows. I hated not to return emails and phone calls. Then there were the requests for styling.

"So I wondered if you'd work with me for a month. On PR. Returning calls and emails about appearances. I want to capitalize on them to help out the business, but I'm not sure which to prioritize."

"I can do that," Toni said. Her eyes were big and brown and the whites very white. Those eyes held intensity and excitement.

"Yeah?"

"Yes, and to prove it to you, I'll give you a month free," Toni said.

The sound of the train from Wells Street caused

Baxy to stir under the table. I felt his soft fur brush against my legs as he poked his head out.

I opened my phone and started counting off the emails and texts and calls I'd gotten over the past weeks. I showed Toni. "You sure?"

"Definitely. Walk me through all this."

I showed her the requests I was getting.

"This is great," she said, still scrolling. "And when the mayor photo runs tomorrow, there will be more."

"So how should we do this?"

"I tell you what. Since I've never done anything in the dog world, I'll give you a month for free. I'll handle your media requests for a month, return the calls and emails, reject the stuff we'd never want to do and run the other things by you."

"And at the end of the month, what happens?"

She shrugged. "You give me a monthly retainer."

Another train rolled by, and the thundering sound stalled any conversation.

Baxter came fully out from under the table then. He gave a great shake, starting with his nose, his head, his shoulders, torso, butt, legs and tail. I had always been envious of a dog's ability to shake off the situation he'd just been in, readying himself for the next. But isn't that what I'd decided I could do, too?

"Sounds good," I said to Toni, raising my glass again. "Let's do it."

16

I woke up, but only very gradually. Color filled in softly around the edges of dark sleep.

Mmmm, I heard myself murmur. I got a flash of thoughts, images, from the deep recesses of my brain. Random scraps of a dream—some kind of beaded ornaments of moments—fell around me, floating.

My eyes slowly opened and then—*bam*—they focused. Everything hit me at once—the blue of his bedroom walls, the reality of him lying at my side.

He was asleep, a light snore emanating from him. Naked and sleeping, he was soft, fresh. Almost too soft?

Sebastian was always unruly in his sleep, turning this way and that, his edges hard, elbows getting me in the leg or gut and then snapping quickly awake whenever he felt a gaze on him.

I looked at Gavin. No, not too soft, I decided. Perfect.

After making out for about four hours, Gavin and
I had damn good sex following a damn good date
that had included an outside beer-tasting at a micro-
brewery on Lincoln Avenue and a symphonic concert in Lincoln Park.

I heard a scratch at the door.

Baxter had slept on the couch, passing out somewhere in the middle of a long French kiss and going
out for a quick walk after. When I opened the door
now, one of his ears was flipped on top of his head,
showing the pearl-pink inside.

He gave me a look. *Are we going home?*

I shook my head. According to a sleek silver clock
on the nightstand, it was only five in the morning.
I leaned forward and ruffled his head. *Go back to
sleep, Baxter.*

He gave a tiny doggy sigh, looked around, then
leaped on the bed.

Gavin mumbled something and turned over. Baxter settled himself into the far corner. He looked at
me, and I could almost hear him saying, *We okay
here? Need me to do anything? Eat his boxer briefs
and regurgitate them? Bark persistently until we're
forced to leave?*

I got back in bed and kissed Bax on the nose. "Go
back to sleep."

Gavin's place was in one of those areas of Chicago that sounded exotic—Wicker Park. There were
a number of art galleries here, which I had always

wanted to see. I'd also heard good things about some boutiques. Still, I only had a vague sense of where I was. Roughly west of Milwaukee Avenue and north of North Avenue? I tried to imagine—when I left here, where would be the best place to get a cab? Or where could I jump on a train?

The questions made me feel unmoored for a second, as if on a suddenly rocking sailboat. Another new place. Another new chapter of life.

Gavin mumbled again in his sleep. I held my breath and leaned in a little. Maybe he'd murmur something about me, something unconscious and yet profound.

I laughed a little when I noticed how excited that thought made me, how fast I'd gone from unmoored to thrilled.

I decided to take the advice I had given my dog. Go back to sleep.

I slipped into dreams that made little sense, that held lots of activity and motion, but always one dog —Baxter—and always one man—Gavin.

When I awoke again, more light was pouring into Gavin's bedroom, making the walls a lighter blue, somehow cloudlike. Gavin was waking, too, eyes blinking drowsily. A small smile. "Hi."

"Hi."

His thumb brushed my lip for a quick moment. "You're pretty."

"Thanks." I wished he would put his thumb back

on my lip. I wished I could lick it or maybe bite it. "You're pretty, too."

He said nothing.

"What?" I said. "Don't like the word *pretty?*"

In one fluid motion, one that was quick and sensual, he had flipped me so that I was looking up at him, his arms behind my lower back, cupping me. "I'm fine with *pretty,*" he said. He bent slowly, slowly, his face coming more into focus. I wouldn't look away from the deep brown of his eyes until they were almost flush with mine. "I'll take *pretty,*" he said. He kissed me. "From you? I'll take anything."

He kissed me again, and he didn't stop.

"I'll make you breakfast," Gavin said an hour later.

He lay next to me, rubbing my arm while I stared at the ceiling, my body rushing, my senses working at hyperspeed. Gavin's smell was lighter than Sebastian's slightly earthy, lavender scent, his skin was softer than Sebastian's, but the memory of him behind me, then over me, then under me, was powerful. Sex with Gavin was more…acrobatic than I'd had with Sebastian, leaving me feeling dizzy. Wonderfully.

"I don't need breakfast," I said, sighing. "I don't need anything."

"C'mon." Gavin edged over to the foot of the bed,

pulled on a T-shirt. "Don't stop me from showing you one of the few skills I have."

"What skill is that?"

"I make the best French toast."

"Really? My dad makes French toast." I leaned against the headboard. He made it for my mother, I told Gavin, her favorite food in the world. As a result, my dad was constantly perfecting the dish.

"Where did you grow up?" he said.

"Saratoga."

"Saratoga Springs, New York?" His voice was excited. "Where they have the Travers Stakes?"

I nodded, smiled. I always loved the week of the Travers horse race—the air filled with excitement, walking in the doors of the track, seeing a sea of women's eclectic bobbing hats.

"I always wanted to go to that race," Gavin said.

"Really?" Sebastian, surprisingly, had never been to a horse race before he met me.

"My grandfather used to take me to the track when we visited him."

"Around here?"

"Yeah. I grew up in a small town a few hours south and we'd go to Arlington."

We talked more about our childhoods, then started to veer into high school years, which was usually cause for me to change the subject.

But we didn't talk of who we dated in high school. We just meandered on memories. As we talked, it was as if a comfortable but exciting emotion began to fill the space between us. He reached a hand out, placed it on the back of my head and gave me the slowest, sweetest kiss. Then he traced my collarbone with the back of his bent index finger. I felt, in the most wonderful way, as if I were being petted. It made me realize how lucky dogs were.

"No disrespect toward your father," he said, "but I'm going to show you that I can kick his French toast's ass."

I laughed. "Well, I'll be the judge of that." I sat up straighter. "I forgot. The picture of Baxy and the mayor is supposed to be in the paper today."

Gavin whooped, causing Baxter to leap to a standing position and give a little warning bark. "Let's go, Baxter!" he said. He looked at me. "You pull it up, and I'll go across the street and get the real paper."

Gavin took a coffee order from me and was soon out the door with the dog.

I decided then to wait for Gavin. I didn't need to see the picture by myself on the phone. I wanted to share it with him.

I lay back on the bed, glad for the moment alone to process my time with Gavin. But my mind kept ushering Sebastian in, which was annoying, so I got out of bed and took my purse into the bathroom, trying to create a makeupless look using lots of makeup. I helped myself to a pair of Gavin's plaid boxers and a T-shirt from a shelf in the bedroom closet.

Gavin's kitchen was small. The walls were painted a light yellow. There was room only for a small table for two. I sat there to let the newness of it all sift through my body.

"Check it out!" Gavin and Baxter rushed through the front door and under the arched doorway into the kitchen. Gavin put down a coffee caddy and dropped three papers on the table. "Front page!" he said.

"You're kidding."

"It's the teaser at the bottom."

My eyes shifted to the bottom of the paper. A cropped picture showed the mayor's smiling face next to Baxter's. Mayor Introduces New First Friend: Superdog!

Inside, the photo of the whole group took up half a page.

No article appeared with it, just the caption. Mayor Mike Flaherty, the first lady, and their three children welcome Superdog and his owner, Jessica Champlin. Ms. Champlin is a stylist now focusing on "dogwear."

I peered closer at the paper, rereading. "Is that a sarcastic quote around the word *dogwear?*" I thought of all the times I'd heard Sebastian muse over grammatical questions while he was working on a piece.

"Who cares?" Gavin said, happily banging pans onto his stove. "You can't *pay* for that advertising. I know. This is my world."

"Seriously," I said. "Tell me the truth. Are they being snarky with the dogwear thing?"

"Seriously, you should write them a thank-you note. That's the single best kind of advertising there is—a huge photo, your name, the type of business you're in." He began whipping eggs. "What are you calling your business, by the way?"

"I'd Rather Sleep with the Dog."

"Ha. I like it. You should be saying that every chance you get. You want it in places like that." He pointed to the paper.

"Good point."

An immense feeling of joy arose then. I loved the feeling of working together, discussing our desires together.

It occurred to me that I couldn't remember feeling joy like that for a long time.

Which brought my mood down a bit. Because I knew joy was often fleeting.

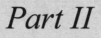

Part II

17

My life was so different than I thought it would be a year ago, than I thought it would be only one month ago, the day the video with Baxter was shot.

Sometimes I peeked backward, through the doorway that was Sebastian and me and wondered what the experience of the Superdog video would have been like if we were still married, but then some contact with him would eliminate such musings. And I thanked the gods I wasn't married to him anymore.

For example, Sebastian had groaned when I'd told him about the shoot with the mayor. He had just returned from another small conflict. "Jesus," he'd said. Then again, *"Jesus."*

I wasn't that irritated, largely because I was still buoyant from seeing Gavin nearly every day.

I cut Sebastian off at the beginning of a diatribe about how he knew he shouldn't have voted for "that idiot Flaherty."

"Hess," I said, barking his last name. That always

made Sebastian snap out of it—barking his name like his coaches used to in high school lacrosse. (He should never have told me that.)

I could feel him glaring over the phone line.

"Do you realize that 'that idiot Flaherty' loves your dog?" I asked. "He said that. *That's* why he wanted his family's picture taken with Baxter. For some reason, they saw something in the video of Baxter that they all loved."

Sebastian went quiet.

I told him how over the past week it had gotten harder to walk down the street. Because within a few days of the mayor photo I knew what it was like to be a celebrity, one who can't walk far before someone wants to greet you. Or at least I knew what it was like to be the celebrity's bodyguard. I couldn't *not* tell Sebastian about this, since he was destined to experience it when he next had Baxy, now that he was back in town.

Because the week the photo was taken had been a particularly slow news week, the mayor of one of the largest cities getting his picture with a dog who had saved a kid was all over the internet, then TV. Because the mayor photo got so much play—it ran on CNN, Fox, MSNBC and the like, all toward the end of the broadcasts, when they needed a pick-me-up before signing off. By the next morning, the videos of Baxter available on the internet had multiplied and it ran on morning shows. And it just kept going.

Hence the difficulty in walking the dog.

"Oh, my God!" was what people usually shouted upon seeing the pup. Another exclamation often followed, usually, "It's Superdog!"

Baxter had always been the type of canine to greet everyone he passed on the street, but now nearly everyone responded. They bent down and petted his head, patted his back. They took photos, then handed their phone to me, asking to take a picture with him.

If we made our way through to Michigan Avenue, the reaction intensified. Baxter was recognized by children and society ladies and young guys in suits alike.

Henry, a guy I eventually learned was a regular at the bar P. J. Clarke's on State and Division, would burst from the doors when we walked by.

"Is that my Baxter?" he would yell. "Is that my Baxy-Baxy?"

The first time it happened I was startled as hell. I didn't know him, and yet he not only bent over and talked to the dog using the *my* adjective, he also scooped Baxter up in his arms and kissed his head. (Baxter just wagged his tail rampantly.) I managed to ascertain that not only had Henry seen the video but he also had met Baxter a number of times with Sebastian, whom he'd known for years.

It was wonderful to see Baxter get so much love. As his "parent" I wanted that for him. To me, Baxter deserved the world, or at least the doggy world, and I wanted to give him the full force of love that I didn't feel from my parents. Even if it involved lots of other people.

The nice thing was Baxter returned love. Simply put, the dog made people happy. Some people would drop to their knees and coo, and their faces, which had appeared strained as they walked toward us, would suddenly lighten and smile. If Baxter had a ball, people wanted to throw it. He would return it to that person for a bit, then seek out someone else. Sometimes he ended up with a coterie of six people vying for him to return the ball to them. Baxter might only have 25 percent of the golden retriever gene in him, but that percentage took over when ball-chasing was involved.

Vinnie, the kid who recorded the video, was getting lots of attention, too (especially from girls at Latin School, he'd told me with a grin). Vinnie called about once a week, asking if he could take Baxter to do "boy things." Best I could tell from watching them from the window, "boy things" meant Vinnie skateboarding and Baxter running alongside him, or Vinnie shooting another video that he put on YouTube, which of course went viral within hours.

One day, I really witnessed the way Baxter affected people. We'd walked past the cardinal's house—a majestic red stone mansion at North Avenue and State—and we crossed the street into the park. Two women were sitting on a bench, one of them hunched over, her hand to her face.

Baxter bounded over and stopped in front of them. He liked to do that, just to say hello.

"Superdog!" the women cried (the one who didn't have her hand to her face). She petted him, but Baxter soon went to the other woman. As I came nearer, I saw she'd been crying. Baxter sat at her feet, his back to her as if to protect her.

"See!" the other woman said. "Superdog loves you, Candace." She looked up at me and said hi.

The woman near Baxter burst into fresh tears. "But I'm a terrible person. How could I do it?"

"Honey, you did it because you loved him."

"But I'm married."

The woman stopped crying and seemed to notice me for the first time. "I'm sorry," she said. "Is this your dog?"

"Yeah."

"He's adorable."

"Thanks."

"I love the Superdog videos."

"Thanks," I said again.

"I'm sorry about this." She waved her hand at her face.

Baxter turned then and stood on his hind paws, putting his front paws on her knees, licking at the tears.

"He's awesome," she said, starting to laugh. "Neither of the men in my life would do this for me."

Her friend guffawed, and soon they were both laughing hard. Soon, they were bent over, howling. It was the kind of laughter that picks up steam and rolls along, the kind of laughter that arises at funerals—that breaks open grief, that tastes like freedom.

But Sebastian didn't love those stories. Of course not.

I cut short my ramblings. "Sorry," I said. "It's not news."

"It's not," he said, his voice low, tense.

"For fuck's sake, Hess."

We both paused for a second. I stifled a laugh. I wasn't sure where that had come from.

"Look," Sebastian said. "It's not like I don't like the idea of Baxy helping someone. I just think it's inappropriate."

"Inappropriate?" I repeated. "In what way?"

Sebastian didn't seem to want to explain that, so he changed the subject.

And that kind of phone exchange put an end to any pining for experiencing the Superdog phenomenon with Sebastian. If I did, I would have had to deal with his issues that the dog video wasn't news, I would have to tone down my enthusiasm. And I didn't want to do that.

18

Luckily, I had a boyfriend who loved the whole Superdog thing. In the few weeks since that first date, Gavin and I had spent so much time together it felt as if we had been dating for months. Our relationship was speeding fast and yet was somehow comfortably thrilling. If we weren't together, we were on the phone or texting.

He'd write, Superdog makes HuffPo! and he'd send me a link. He watched with the same awe I did when people descended on Baxter and especially when he made them happy.

"He's the Jesus Christ of dogs," Gavin said one day when a group of serious-looking Japanese tourists seemingly became children again, lying on the sidewalk with Baxter.

We'd spent those nights mostly in his cozy kitchen, the yellow walls surrounding us, the Wilco music he often played bouncing off them. We worked on our laptops or I brought over collar or leash samples to work on and show him.

Often, we'd fill in the blanks of our lives from before we'd met each other.

"She was cool," Gavin said one night, answering my questions about his ex-girlfriend of three years. He took a couple of Stella beers out of the fridge and opened them for us, placing them on the table. "She still is cool."

"So what happened?" I took a sip, the beer tasting icy cold and fresh.

"I loved her," he said. Nothing after that.

"Were you *in* love with her?"

He shook his head. "I wanted to be."

"Hmm." I took another sip. "Sometimes I wished I wasn't in love with my ex-husband." I stopped. "Back then," I added.

"What do you mean? What happened with you guys?"

I told him why Sebastian and I weren't together— because of his job, because I couldn't live with the not knowing where he was and when he'd be home.

"It was impossible to plan anything," I said.

"Yeah, that would be tough. I understand why you didn't want to do it."

"It's not that I didn't want to. I *couldn't*." This seemed an important point to emphasize.

Gavin nodded. Then he looked sheepish.

"What?" I said.

He leaned back against the counter, looking down at me while I sat at his small kitchen table. "I have to make a confession."

"Okay."

"I read some of Sebastian's work."

"Yeah?" I was amused, nothing else.

"I wanted to see if he was a good writer."

"And?"

"And he's a freaking great writer."

"I know."

"And he loves his work." Gavin's words had a heaviness.

"Yes." *I just wish he had loved me as much as the job.*

"Lucky bastard."

Gavin poured out his frustrations with his own job. He talked about calling on accounts—how those he knew would advertise were just as boring to call on as trying to get new accounts.

"It's all so meaningless," he said, "ad space in magazines." He made a derisive sound. "I could be selling apples. Or toilet seats."

"Can't you try to make it meaningful? I mean what about approaching accounts that you think deserve some advertising and fight to give them breaks? Or what about moving into a different area of the company?"

Gavin groaned. "Doesn't really work that way."

"What about trying to get on the editorial side?"

"Ha. It *really* doesn't work that way."

"But you wish it did?"

He looked at me for a beat, and then he looked down at the table. "Yeah, I wish I'd started out there. I wish I'd gotten a journalism degree rather than a business degree." He shrugged. "But I didn't. So this is the job I have now."

"So change it. You can. I did. I feel like I've been coming alive in the past few weeks. It's really possible to change."

"It's okay, Jess." He leaned in and kissed me slowly. "I like my life a lot better now that I met you."

I smiled big. I stood up and put my arms around him.

The next night, Gavin made me pasta. He mixed flour and eggs and water. He put the dough through a machine that he hand-cranked, rolling out ribbons. He was so proud of that pasta.... He was adorable.

Baxter went wherever Gavin went, sitting at his feet, waiting for him to occasionally let him sample some sausage. Gavin and I drank from a bottle of Alto Adige, a white Italian wine. We kissed often and well. We spoke about everything, slipping from one conversation to another with ease.

"So, will you have kids?" Gavin asked.

It was the first time I'd felt a slowage in the conversation that night.

He noticed it, too, apparently. He raised his hands as if in surrender. "Is that not a good question?"

I pulled my glass to me. "It's a completely legitimate question. And one everyone wants to talk about. I noticed that during my brief attempt to fill out an online dating profile."

He laughed. "Yeah, I've dated online. It's an experience. Did you do it at all?"

I shook my head no. "I read some of the responses. There were a couple hundred. I got overwhelmed."

Gavin looked thoughtful. "It's kinda nice, filling out the profile and all that. Because you figure out what you want. But getting specific like that, I worried I was missing out on meeting some really cool people."

I didn't really relish the thought of Gavin with other people, but I didn't say anything.

"But it's weird," he continued, "because you go on these dates with these women, and you already know so much about the person from the profile and emailing back and forth."

Definitely didn't like the thought of him with other women.

"So anyway. What if *we* were on a date," he said, "say, after meeting online…"

He looked sheepish again.

I finished for him. "You would know, already, that I'm undecided on the whether-to-have-kids front."

Growing up, I'd never been sure whether I wanted children. Being an only child myself, I knew what loneliness was, even before I'd given the feeling a name. And in my parents' world, I knew what it felt like to not belong. So I only wanted kids if I knew I was 100 percent committed, if I knew I was ready to work to make them never feel lonely.

"Okay," Gavin said. He nodded.

"And what would I know about you on that front?"

"I want kids." He said it so immediately, in such an assured way, that for some reason I felt an ache in the center of me.

"You sound pretty confident about that."

He shrugged. "It's something I've always known." He slid his hand across the table, covering mine. "But I'm open to anything, to different decisions."

"Me, too."

He squeezed my hand then. "Especially if it's with the right person."

"Exactly."

I turned my hand over and braided my fingers with his. A doorway to a different life appeared.

I took Baxter out for a walk while Gavin boiled water, and that was when I got another glimpse of another doorway. Walking the dog up Cortland Avenue, I missed the dog park, which Bax and I hadn't seen much of lately. But right behind that missing was a big expanse in my mind. It felt as if it were shining with clarity. Yes, I missed things about my past lives, regretted things about my past lives, but I knew I was in an entirely new one. I was hyperaware of my surroundings. And I started asking myself questions. *What if I (we) lived on this street or near it? Would I go to that bar sometimes, that restaurant?* I turned a corner and there was a boutique. *Would I shop there?* Across the street, a doggy bakery. *Would Baxter get hooked on some canine cookie that I would give him only for special occasions?* I saw a yoga studio. *Maybe I'll finally get into yoga. Maybe I'll learn there.*

I could envision all of those things. They were all doorways into different worlds, ones that could be reached, hypothetically, by continuing a relationship with someone I now adored, by maybe moving to his neighborhood that was only a few miles from my own.

Later that night, Gavin and I had sex in his bedroom while Baxter snoozed on the living room couch. "Had sex" sounds so vague, but it was anything but. Gavin was such a sweet, delicious kisser. He liked to make out for a long time, hands straying to my breasts, then disappearing, then later his fingers briefly touching me between my legs, then also going away. He was a tease. He liked to kiss me until he was taunting me with those fingers, those hands. I would try to unbutton his shorts, wanting to release the obvious straining, but he'd say no. Eventually, I would ask. Or I would beg. Or I would stand and slowly take off any clothes I still had on. And then he would give himself to me.

Sometimes when he was inside me he was rough, but in a delicious way, causing me to arch into him. His desire for me seemed intensely charged, as if it would never abate. It set me on fire, made my flesh hot, my face flush.

After, under a tent of cotton sheets, he lay curled around me, gentle again, and we talked. My eyes were closed, and I felt as if I was floating, floating through the future, to the places Gavin and I might go together, emotionally and physically. Maybe we would continue to date and we would travel to Vietnam. Maybe we'd pick up sailing. Maybe we'd love it so much we'd buy a boat and get a slip at Monroe Harbor (a place that always looked magical when I sped by it in a cab). Maybe we'd start hanging out at the yacht club. Maybe we'd meet fascinating people and have a whole new circle of friends.

I pushed myself back into the curve of Gavin's body.

Baxter came into the room and decided to jump from the floor to the bed, landing apparently right on Gavin, who made an *oof* sound. I heard him laugh, knew the dog was probably licking his ear.

Baxter walked over the two of us and tucked himself into my chest, his back to me. He curled into himself until he was just a coil of golden fur. I put my hand on his flank and we lay there like that— Gavin, his arm draped over my hip and me, with my hand on Baxy's side. I nestled back into Gavin more.

Just then, the doorway to the other world seemed larger, huge. And I could just about imagine myself walking through it.

19

Business started to boom. I've always wanted to be able to say something like that. *My business is booming.* As a stylist, unless you're in the celeb side of the business (one who lands a client who is constantly on a red carpet) it can be a very swinging business—up and forth and down and back.

But with all the publicity around Baxter, my dog-wear line got hot, just like the temperatures—July sliding into August's humidity. I still wasn't making a lot of money yet because I was spending cash to try out different manufacturers, purchase materials and work on a website. I'd officially hired Toni as a publicist only three weeks into our trial run. She had gotten the mayor photo into many media and she'd also gotten an article about Baxter and me in a national women's magazine. She'd then gotten me and Baxter booked for three well-paid speaking engagements which were just five minutes of talking and forty minutes of Baxter (and sometimes Baxter and me) getting our photos taken. And last but not least, after my unsatisfactory searches, she'd found me a small manufacturing facility in Grand Rapids, Michigan, and a sourcing director who knew how to get dogwear materials much cheaper and faster than I did. They worked fast and produced great products.

I was working so much that for the first time in my life I was sleeping only about five hours a night. I was exhausted. And also joyously bewildered.

And then I took a leap. I rented a studio on Wells Street.

The studio was above a cigar shop, which was apparently why they'd had trouble renting it—everyone assumed that it would reek of smoke. But the scent was minimal, a spicy waft that gave the place an exotic feel. My agent made a lowball offer after I told her I loved the hardwood floors and black-painted ductwork. We were both surprised when they accepted. I purchased scaled containers for the supplies, and every morning, Bax and I walked down State Street to the park, then down North Avenue, past the corner of North and Clark, the very corner where Baxter saved a kid only a month and a half ago.

Baxter was a trouper. He had become more spirited, and yet somehow more mature, since the whole viral video began. Eventually, I started seeing Baxter as my business partner—which is really what he was. Before that, I would sometimes get irritated with him while I was trying to work. When he stuck his black button nose (for the thirtieth time) into the basket of ribbons I was working with and started to chew, I would grow annoyed and gently shove him away. But after I rented the studio and gave him partner status, I changed my approach to a more grateful one. After all, Baxter had in some ways led me into the new life I was enjoying.

And Baxter was gracious since he realized that to submit to my wrapping of ribbon and fabric around him led to praise and treats.

One of the first items I made in the studio, I made for Sebastian. Or rather for Baxter to wear when he was with Sebastian. It was a black leather jacket, definitely for a male dog, with a stitched crucifix on the back. It was huge with the Harley crowd and was selling the best in Arizona and Nevada.

But I didn't have much time after that to design for Baxter. Local celebs started consulting with me when they were thinking of getting a puppy. Those calls led me to creating the Puppy Starter Kit, with two collars, one leash, a couple of add-ons for collars (like flower clips for girls) and a dog bed. Originally, I gave them as new puppy gifts to people who'd consulted with me. When Victory finally caved to her kids and agreed to a second dog, I threw her a puppy shower and two magazines covered it. Soon "puppy shower" started to be checked more and more as a reason for purchase on my site, and my Puppy Starter Kits were selling like crazy.

Eventually, I trusted Baxter more and more for his reaction to things I was working on. I watched his reaction to a collar, a leash. If he seemed to like the item then I immediately called my manufacturer in Grand Rapids. Suddenly, I had a muse for my dog-wear. My dog.

Sebastian texted me that he'd just gotten through customs. I was surprised. He'd only been gone a week. Another short trip.

I texted him, Welcome back.

I looked at Gavin, who was sitting on my couch across from me. We decided to spend some time at my place which was closer to the studio. Would he care that I was texting with my ex? I wondered. Now that it was clear Gavin and I were officially dating, did I have to tell him things like that?

I got up and walked to the kitchen.

Sebastian texted again. Get Baxy now?

I stood in the kitchen, not doing anything.

Sebastian must have sensed from my delay that I wasn't quite ready to give Baxter up (even though I'd had him for over a week, and Sebastian had a right to see him).

Sorry, he wrote. Not a lot of notice.

I texted back, No problem. But I might need to take him to the studio at least once this week.

I turned when Gavin came into the kitchen.

He opened the refrigerator. "I'm hungry. Feel like getting an early dinner?"

"Sebastian is coming to get the dog."

"Baxter's leaving?" he said, closing the door. Baxter came into the room and looked at the kitchen, immediately dropping into his "sit and wait for food" position.

"Oh, Baxter," Gavin said. He scooped up the dog in his arms, letting him lick his ear. "I'll miss ya, buddy."

"Let's get something to eat after he comes by," I said.

"Great," Gavin said. "Do you… Do you want me to get out of here?"

"No," I answered quickly.

"You're ready for me to meet your ex-husband?" He said it in an almost jokey tone, but the question had a weight to it.

I certainly wasn't going to ask Gavin to wait in my room, so there were two options: introduce him to Sebastian or tell him I'd meet him at a restaurant.

Gavin put Baxter on the floor and took treats out of his pocket, making him do basic commands—sit, down, shake. Baxter, who still adored Gavin, did anything he asked. Watching him, I knew how the dog felt. I adored him, too.

And really, what was the big deal with my ex-husband? I was dating and it was that simple.

"Stay," I said to Gavin, as if I were giving him a command, too.

He smiled, gave a brief nod of his head.

When a knock sounded at the door, Gavin and I were in my small living room. It was a room I rarely used, and lately it had become Gavin's place where he read magazines and watched sports.

"I'll just let him know you're here," I said. "Before I make introductions."

"Gotcha," he said. "See you in a minute."

I hustled to the door and opened it for Sebastian. I started to tell him Gavin was there, but something about the look he was giving me stopped me.

"I missed you," Sebastian said.

"Oh," I said, taken aback. "Thanks…"

I was saved by Baxter tearing into the room, giving a high, happy bark.

"Dogger!" Sebastian said, kneeling to pet him briefly before standing back up.

The features of his face, his jaw, his neck seemed softer than usual. His gaze was unguarded, maybe sentimental.

"How was your trip?" I asked, not to bug him, but really because he looked a little upset.

He exhaled. "Okay." He shook his head a little, opening his eyes wider, as if trying not to see some image in his head.

"Really. Are you okay?" I asked.

Something tensed in him. "Sure. Of course."

"Okay." I paused. "I just wanted to tell you that I have a friend over."

"Oh."

"And we're heading to dinner when you leave… when you and Bax are gone, so…" Why was I having such a hard time coming up with words? "I just wanted to give you a heads-up that he's here."

"He?"

I heard footsteps behind me. "Hey, man," Gavin said. He crossed the kitchen, appearing at my side, and held out a hand.

"Sebastian, this is Gavin Medlin," I said. "Gavin, Sebastian Hess." I sounded exactly like my dutiful seven-year-old self when my mom used to make me practice introductions before the annual Travers Stakes festivities where I would meet many adults. And I felt as if I was about seven right then with Gavin and Sebastian. Despite the fact that I had shared some of the most intimate (physically and otherwise) moments with these two men, I wanted to both hide in a closet and giggle inappropriately.

"Yeah, man, I've read some of your stuff and I love it," Gavin said.

A pause before I heard Sebastian say, "Thanks."

"You're a great writer."

"Thanks a lot," Sebastian said, sounding only vaguely genuine. "Are you a writer?"

"No, I'm in sales."

"Ah," Sebastian said. It sounded haughty, though

I knew that didn't mean he meant to sound that way. Sebastian had always been flummoxed by people with vague-sounding jobs. *A consultant?* he would say to me as we discussed people we met at a party. *What does that mean? They could be a consultant for any company! How about a little detail?* The writer in Sebastian was always on the hunt for good details.

Sebastian murmured something to Gavin, something that sounded like, "Good for you," which sounded even more haughty, although I knew he was just trying to back out of the conversation. He was saved by Baxter who yelped again and jumped at Sebastian's feet until he picked him up, exactly as Gavin had earlier.

"Gavin is in ad sales," I said, which drew a glare from Gavin. I closed my mouth to make sure I didn't add that Gavin worked for an a celebrity-driven magazine.

Silence.

The conversation was going nowhere fast.

Sebastian turned to the brass pegs hanging on the wall, "I'll just grab a leash," he said, reaching out for the brown one with a practiced hand. The gold-starred leash hung there, too. Sebastian seemed to pause and grimace at it, but I could have imagined that.

"Anything else I need for this one?" he said, his head nodding toward the dog.

"Oh, he's got that eye infection again. Let me get

the drops." I turned to the pantry and opened it, but as I rooted around, unable to find them, I felt the need to attempt easier conversation. "The vet said it probably keeps coming back because he meets so many people now."

"Yeah. He never gets those infections except when he's with you."

I turned to see Sebastian looking not at me, but at Gavin.

"Um…" I said, no good reply.

Sebastian glanced at me then. "The drops?"

"One second."

I took off toward my bathroom at a clip, straining my ears. Nothing. No sounds from the kitchen. I snagged the drops from the drawer.

"Look, man," Gavin was saying when I was nearly in the kitchen. A low voice. I stopped.

"Would you quit calling me 'man'?" Sebastian said.

"Look, I'm just saying it would be nice if you gave her a little heads-up. I know what she needs."

"What who needs?" I said, stepping into the room.

"You," Gavin answered fast. "I was telling him to give you more time when he's picking up the dog."

"And I told him," Sebastian said, "that he could butt out of my marriage."

Sebastian and I looked at each other, all of us silent. *Did he just say, "My marriage"? As in present tense?*

I've never been able to stand the alpha male thing that some guys did—*She's my girl; I'll protect her.* But hell if it wasn't kinda sexy the way Gavin's chest grew higher, straining toward Sebastian. And oddly, I felt a kind of pride at Sebastian's word-slip.

But none of us seemed to want to address it. I wasn't even positive that Sebastian noticed he'd said it.

Then Baxter barked. We all looked down.

My muse, my partner, my friend, the dog stood at my feet, his back to me in protection, barking at the two men and showing them who the alpha was around here.

20

The next TV piece on Baxter was on a national news magazine, and it started like most personal-interest news stories, showing the video that had gotten so much attention. Then they talked about Baxter, then about Clara and how the little girl was thriving. Next, the piece reviewed me as Baxter's owner and the one who'd sewn the stars on his collar and leash.

Jessica Champlin, the voice-over said, *had been a stylist for many years before her dog, Baxter, struck fame.* The video showed me crouching, feeding Baxter a treat, then kissing him on the head. *She had built a successful business in Manhattan before relocating to Chicago. She styles not only entertainment and news personalities* (a still photo of Pamela at the news desk) *but socialites and politicians, as well* (video of me considering a purple suit on Victory).

Champlin will even make clothes for clients when she can't find what she wants commercially (cue video of me at my sewing machine). *But it wasn't*

*until her dog was caught on video with his Superdog
collar and leash, which Champlin had created, that
she realized there was a market for dog styling and
products, or, as she calls it, "dogwear."*

A segment followed with an interview with me,
the background showing my kitchen windows and a
choppy, gray-blue Lake Michigan beyond. "If there's
womenswear and menswear," I said in the video,
"why not dogwear?"

The next few shots were of me and Baxter walking outside, then of my studio, where Baxter went
right to his side of the worktable to eat from his bowl.

They showed a clip of me talking about how the
Superdog collar had started as a way to rib my ex.

And then my ex was in the video. *In* the video.
There were Sebastian and I outside my building
under sunny skies, Sebastian handing me Baxy's
leash, smiling at me.

The shot appeared an easygoing one. But it had
not, in any way, been simple to get Sebastian to
agree.

I'd finally broached the subject of him being on
camera a few nights later when I met him outside to
hand Baxy over to him. He was late for a dinner at
his mom's house in Roger's Park.

"Ha. Sorry, babe," he'd said when I finally asked
if he would be in the video. He scoffed.

That scoff. It made me not want to back down.

It made me want to squeeze him into doing what I wanted.

"C'mon," I said, my voice tight. "The producers of the show like the 'joint custody' thing."

"What joint custody thing?"

"*Our* thing." I cleared my throat. "*You* were the one that first called it that. Now they say it's a trend."

"Oh, Jesus. We're trending?"

"Joint custody of pets is trending. It won't be forever. This whole thing will be over soon. But right now it's bringing me business. That I happen to love. So do me a freaking favor!"

I wondered how he would react to the anger that had bubbled up with that last sentence. Outbursts, even short ones, weren't usually in my nature.

The summer weather seemed to envelop our little pocket of silence. The sun was slipping over the city to the west. You could tell it was deep in the summer, too, because the *zing-zing* of cicadas could be heard.

Then Sebastian stepped forward and tucked a piece of hair behind my right ear. I froze. That was what he used to do. When we were married. When we were happy.

Did he smell Gavin on me? I suddenly wondered. I'd showered since last night, but in more ways than one Gavin had become a part of me over the past few weeks, and I wondered if maybe he'd gotten in my pores a little, if Sebastian could detect him somehow.

My loyalty to Gavin was there, making me want

to pull away from my ex. But I sensed opportunity. And I also wanted Sebastian to *want* to do something. So I stayed there. I moved in a little closer. "Do this for me," I said, "okay?"

"No way, Jess."

But he hadn't moved away.

A couple from my building (formerly *our* building) passed us with cheery hellos. Although we shared the same address, we obviously kept different schedules because I hadn't seen them in forever, which was even more self-evident when they invited Sebastian and me over for "drinks sometime," clearly thinking we were still together.

When they'd left, neither of us trying to explain our vague responses, Sebastian looked at me.

"Seriously, Jess," he said, "I will *not* be on camera."

"Why not?"

"I can't."

"Won't."

"Can't."

"Says who?"

"This is ridiculous. We've been over this."

I didn't respond. I moved in a little closer again, and then I added in a small voice, "Please."

He exhaled with irritation. "No."

"Please."

"No."

"This is the last time I'll ask, the last time I'll try

to talk you into something. This is for my business."
I didn't add that his business had caused the end of
us. We both knew that script well enough.

"Okay," he said into my ear then, his breath hot.
Surprisingly, it sent tingles down my insides, through
my limbs.

I turned my head a little, and now I could smell
his jaw and his neck—the slightly lavender shav-
ing cream, the Sebastian smell, deep and woodsy
yet clean.

"Okay?" I said into his ear.

"I'll do it," Sebastian said.

Then we both stepped back.

And so the shooting of the video went well, and
the arrangement between Sebastian and me came up
at the end of the piece.

Joint custody of the dog? the reporter's voice-over
said in closing. *It may not be for everyone but these
two are making it work. For themselves and for Superdog.* (Per Sebastian's insistence, they didn't use
his name or his occupation.)

My parents saw the news piece and called me
the next day.

"So you and Sebastian might be getting back together?" my mom asked. "That's what it looked like
from the video."

The video had not, in any way that I could see,
made it appear as if reconciliation was an option.
So I quickly denied, and then moved on by telling

my parents about the Wells Street studio. My father whooped, and my mother gave her delighted bird laugh.

They asked me question after question about my dogwear, eventually moving on to questions about design. "Are your designs inspired by art?" they asked me. "Or a particular designer?"

I thought hard about what to say. *Were they hoping I'd name a piece of art of theirs?* They often asked this question and naming one of their creations was a favored answer. But they always pushed for more, as if they knew it couldn't only be them who influenced me. I don't think they realized they influenced me much more than they knew.

I thought about it.

"Well, there's one girl dog collar that's made up of tiny red butterflies. I drew from Alexander McQueen."

"Oh?" my father said.

"Tell us more," my mom said.

I talked about how I loved the headdress McQueen had made with red butterflies.

"I can see that," my mother said. "I see you aligned with McQueen, God rest his soul. You're both artists."

That was how my parents talked. I didn't always like that, but now my heart puffed with pride and love.

And yet I didn't give Baxter credit for being my muse. I felt bad for that later in the day when the

worst happened. Then I felt like I had betrayed him.
But I loved being close to my parents in that way on
the phone—talking creatively, bonding (however
slightly), that I didn't want to miss a minute of it.

21

A quietly bouncing ball can change everything. That's what I learned that day.

I'd Rather Sleep with the Dog had gotten into the ball business via Brent, the sourcing consultant at the Michigan manufacturing plant. I was happy about it since it involved no design for me, just deciding where to put the I'd Rather Sleep with the Dog logo. But even better, Baxter—my muse, my test subject—loved not just chasing balls, but retrieving them and racing back to drop them at your feet. If he misjudged and the drop of his ball hit a foot away from your foot, he'd pick it up and readjust so you wouldn't have to move your feet to throw it.

And so as the boxes of sample dog balls continued to arrive at my condo and studio, Baxter was in canine nirvana. He got to try each—a tennis ball that was purple and more durable, a metallic silver one that seemed entirely too big for Baxter's mouth, a red one that had holes all over its hard, rubbery surface. There were many with bells, many more that emanated squeaks—from dainty cooing ones to screeching death metal.

His favorite, the one he liked to hold in his mouth and trot with around our neighborhood, was one that a rubber company had forwarded to Brent. It was lime-green with rubber spikes. And Baxter liked to mouth it even more than the one with the holes.

Baxter loved to hold that ball up high as he walked, showing it to people as he passed. People often laughed, pointed. Even when they recognized and shouted "Superdog" they rarely approached when he held the ball like that, as if they could tell from Baxter's posture and countenance that he wasn't to be interrupted. It was hysterical. It was always a mood picker-upper for me.

But then that day.

That day. That day. That's how I would refer to it later. Just a vague description of one twenty-four-hour period.

That day it was blazing hot by the time Baxter and I got outside. That day, we set out on a walk, Baxter holding his green ball. That day, a Newfoundland suddenly appeared, full bark, at the fence of a grand house on East Scott Street, startling Baxter. That day, the ball bounced from his mouth, just a small bounce. That day, Baxter yanked away from me, his DNA taking over, a dog dashing for his favorite ball.

"Baxter!" I yelled. "Stay!"

But he went.

"Baxter!"

That moment froze and then I wasn't there; instead I was in a field of black and I saw flashes, tiny pockets of memories exploding all at once—*pop, pop, pop, pop, pop.* Each flash was like a camera burst on the red carpet, but each flash was its own microburst of a world.

And like a photograph or a video, I could see each one of them—Baxy at different stages of his life: Baxter as a ragamuffin puppy with adoring eyes who almost never got to walk because Sebastian and I couldn't stop carrying him; later, Baxter streaking across the park, looking over one shoulder while Sebastian yelled, *Go long!* to his dog-son; Baxter, the good sport, finding joy in a squeaky toy he hadn't seen for a week because he'd been at Sebastian's, shuffled back and forth because we both loved him so much; Baxter on TV; Baxter making people happy on the street; Baxter in our studio, twisted up in a coil of yellow collar leather.

And then the real moment was back.

"Baxter!"

It was rush hour, and I heard other pedestrians on the street yelling, too. Then a car was barreling toward Baxter, who was in the middle of the street. The squeal of brakes as the car swerved, almost hitting a biker.

I shrieked his name over and over.

A leash streamed behind Baxter, but not the one with the golden stars. He was not Superdog, not anymore. He wore only a plain navy collar and leash. He was just a dog....

The first car had missed Bax, but now an SUV—*wham!*

Then quiet.

Then screaming.

22

At the pet hospital, a reality show played, loud, in the waiting room.

Me. Just me.

I hadn't taken my phone with me on our walk because I was only going a few blocks.

That was one of the things I said over and over to everyone— *we were just on a walk, needed a break. he was carrying his ball, it's not a crowded street, I don't have my phone.* I wound through and repeated those points to the receptionist at the front desk, then the next receptionist who took over from her, then the nurse who took him away, then the vet who came out to look for a different dog owner, then the same vet when she came out to tell me she had no news (and who grimaced and touched my shoulder), then to myself because they felt like "normal" sentences now, and I could think of nothing else.

I wanted to think about things from the weeks before the accident. I wanted to think about the Superdog video and the press and the new studio and Gavin and "dogwear" and the mayor. That time, though chaotic in its own way, had developed into a particular status quo, one that now seemed normal, innocent, sweet.

But I just kept talking about what had happened immediately before the accident, about how *I'd taken Baxter for a walk by myself. I needed a break from work, and then the accident happened. I didn't take my phone with me because I was only going a few blocks.*

But after three hours, the sentences were instilled so deeply in me I didn't need to repeat them mantra-like. I sat on the brown couch, staring blankly at the hospital TV showing that reality show. The normalcy (that I hadn't realized was normal) faded. Then, I could only see the accident. I could think only of how the person in the SUV had peeled off after the crash, after I'd run toward him, reached under the car and dragged Baxter out in my arms.

Baxter had been shaking violently. He cried and cried, and those cries cut into me. I watched the SUV screech away. I began to shake as much as my dog.

A woman on the street—Marilyn Miles, she said her name was; I will never forget that name, Marilyn Miles—drove us to the hospital in her car, which was parked right there. Baxter trembled and mewled painfully the whole way.

That mewling hung like a low cloud in the back of my mind at the hospital, playing constantly.

Marilyn Miles had stayed with me for a while, letting me use her cell phone. My brain was scrambled. Sebastian's number was one of the few I could remember without seeing my contacts. I called him. I knew he was in town, yet his phone was off. My jumbled mind still recalled that sometimes Sebastian turned off the phone when he was deep into research, usually preparing for another trip. I couldn't bear to text him until I had news. I didn't want anyone, even my ex-husband, to feel as bad as I did in that hospital.

I didn't know Gavin's number by heart. I'd saved it in my phone the day we met and had never given the actual numbers much thought.

On the brown couch I kept looking from the TV toward the double doors through which they'd taken Baxy, the doors through which the vet said she would return.

The waiting room resembled a doctor's waiting room, but when those tall doors swung open I saw a cavernous, silver space beyond, like a long tube leading to a research lab. I read the brochure for the hospital, my eyes misting over the descriptions— *operating rooms, trauma, ICU.*

Hang tight, the vet had said. She looked just like a young doctor on a TV show. Pretty. But I also read grave concern in her features and in the way she touched me on the shoulder. I knew my thinking could be off, but the way I read it, she was worried about my dog.

When Marilyn Miles had left (hugging me, giving me her business card with her home phone number written on it) the receptionist had said I could use their phone if needed. But who to call other than Sebastian? What other numbers did I know from memory? It was shameful how few.

I thought of my parents. I knew their number, of course. They'd had the same one since I was a kid. What I didn't know was how they would respond to a crisis. If history foretold anything, not so well.

My arrest. I tried never to think about it, had mostly succeeded in that amnesic endeavor since it happened. But it crept up once in a while. Especially then in the pet hospital, for some reason.

I put my head back on the couch, not caring about the awkward cocked angle of my neck, and my past zoomed in, as if the trauma with Baxter had ripped the doors off the memory.

When the cops rang the doorbell at the apartment I shared with Billy, they identified themselves, and I not only let them in, I grabbed my bag and told them to take me. Before I got in the car they read the Miranda rights. I kept nodding quickly for them to get it over with, not because I was so mortified to be on the street and being arrested (which I was) but because a small voice was already talking. *It had to happen. Good...good.*

But it wasn't good when Billy came to see me, dragging his eyes up and down the khaki prisoner jumpsuit I wore.

"This has got to end, Jess," he said. "We can't have this kind of publicity."

"This kind of publicity?" I said. "This kind of publicity?" I repeated that a few more times. *This kind of publicity.*

"Jess…listen to me."

"You know your brother Mick asked me to pick up that package."

"Those *drugs,*" Billy said, as if he had never used. As if I ever had.

"Yeah," I said. "It was your brother who asked me to pick up those *drugs*. He wanted this to happen."

Billy, the only one who'd always been there for me, the one I had blindly assumed would always be there for me, shook his head and walked away.

And it certainly didn't get any better when my parents found out. I suppose their response was one many a parent would have—suggestions of inpatient treatment, when I needed none; threats of involuntary hospitalization, pleas combined with begging. They were confused. I wasn't.

So I didn't call my parents from the pet hospital. I finally lifted my head and stared lifelessly ahead, and then I sat and sat and sat on the brown sofa, watching the reality show. I saw the show from a distance—in some sliver of my mind still processing data, refusing to shade it, almost as if I was recording it.

The show was about a pack of traveling fashion models. They were in an Austrian-looking place, at a photo shoot. A huge chessboard, the pieces chest-high, served as their set. The models lounged on the pieces, draping arms over a knight, kicking out a long beautiful leg. When they spoke you realized they were teenage girls from various towns in the U.S., sounding like teenage girls do.

After Austria, another episode began.

I looked toward the front desk at the second receptionist who was video-chatting with a friend, no other patients or clients around. I thought about asking her for the remote because the show was reminding me of my styling business and that was reminding me of Baxter. But I couldn't seem to move.

The next episode was set in Spain. Dully, I watched.

"Baxter's mom?" Another youngish woman in a doctor's coat, arms wrapped around a clipboard.

I stood fast, glancing at the doors that were swinging shut behind her. How had I missed that they had opened?

"I'm Dr. Kasha," the woman said. I read her name tag: Brittany Kasha DVM.

I looked around. "But another doctor took Baxter."

"Yes, I just came on shift. I've been here for most

of the exam and tests, and I took over for Dr. Parsons."

I tried to process what she was saying, which I knew, logically, was simple enough information. Over Dr. Kasha's head, tears streaked down the face of a teenage girl, one of the models without makeup.

"You're Baxter's mom, right?"

Baxter's mom. Baxter's mom. Baxter's mom.

"I'm Baxter's mom."

I knew her eyes were searching my face. I saw that. Normally, I would have tried to compose myself. I was unable. *Baxter's mom. Baxter's mom. Baxter's mom.*

"Let's sit," she said.

Right there, on the brown couch, we sat. Another sliver of my mind opened—analytical but reckless, guessing at outcomes in the hopes of preparing myself. *Was it good she was delivering news in the waiting room? Or was it so dire that they couldn't let me even see Baxy?*

Prep for the worst, some voice in my mind said. Then it answered itself with a question. *How? How?* I heard the sound of Baxter mewling. My eyes shot to the silver doors. Closed. Was that sound in my head?

"So," Dr. Kasha said, "let's review what we've found so far." She unclasped the clipboard and looked at it.

I looked around. No mewling dog. I was still

the only one in the waiting room besides Brittany Kasha, DVM.

The vet ran through test results—no signs of internal bleeding, no obvious fractures "…that we can tell." She kept saying that.

…*That we can tell. Right now.*

"Also…"

I heard that word when she said it, so distinct, followed by a pause.

"Also, Baxter's BUN is elevated." Another pause.

"I don't know what that means," I said.

"It means we're concerned about kidney damage, possibly perforation."

"B-U-N," I repeated, trying to learn, trying to join all the voices in my head—the observer, the processer, the guesser, the mewler, the logician, the one who wanted to remember leaving for a walk without my phone, when it was all normal.

I felt dizzy. "Where is Baxter?"

"We have him in ICU."

Not good, not good.

"Also…" she said. That word again. "Initially, there were no signs of a concussion, but now we notice a red spot on his eye. Could be he just took a hit there, but…"

I squeezed my eyes shut and the flashes came, the memory bursts—the feel of Baxter's ears and the two and a half pounds of him when we drove home the day we got him. Baxter streaking across the dog beach at Montrose. Baxter running across the park to Sebastian. Baxter when he was Superdog. When he was still Superdog. When.

Then Baxter running into the street. *Wham!*

Dr. Brittany Kasha continued to talk, sounding young, not like the models on the TV above her head exactly, but not too far, either.

She started explaining more about the kidney perforation, not calling it possible anymore, just saying, "the kidney perforation." And then I heard "…could be fatal."

No, no, no, no, no, no, no, no, no, no, no, no, no.

I realized the word *no* said over and over wasn't in my mind. It was my voice, and I would not stop saying it.

23

There was, with a dog, a finite end to the relationship. And that end was different than with a human being, in that it usually came quicker. Dogs lived maybe ten to fifteen years, I'd been told. Shortly before the accident, I had received an email from a customer who said of her dog, Pepper and I had twenty years together. Well, nineteen years and seven months. Even after he died, I bought him your star collar and leash, because Pepper was a star. My star. And everything dimmed after his passing.

That email slayed my emotions. Unless you got your dog when you were eighty years old (or some such) you were likely to outlive it. And never did I hear someone discussing the loss of a beloved pet and say, "Eh, it wasn't so bad." Never did I hear anyone say that such a death was anything but profoundly sad.

Baxter came into my life in my thirties, and so I had this vague concept (call it a subtle awareness) that I would have him, maybe, until the end of my forties.

Sitting in the pet hospital, my forties loomed.

I could hear my life passing, which meant Baxy's was passing even faster.

Tick, tick, tick.

I stood and tried to shake the way Baxter did, whether he was shaking off the rain or a stressful moment. It kinda worked. But I still needed to call him. Sebastian. As much as I wanted to shield him if possible, I couldn't handle this alone. Plus he deserved to know—he loved Baxter as much as I did, if that was even possible.

I walked to the front desk and asked the receptionist if I could make a call. She slid the phone across the high, white counter.

"I love you, Baxter."

No response from my dog. It had been only twenty minutes since I left Sebastian a message, but it felt like twenty years of waiting.

They'd finally let me through the silver doors to see him. It led to a hallway, much less imposing than I'd imagined, and for some reason I found myself disappointed at the banality of it. They couldn't say when Baxter might leave, or even if he might leave. They wanted to watch his BUN levels, assess him for concussion and have him seen by an orthopedist the next day. Dr. Kasha had received "unfortunate news" from a radiologist who reread the X-rays, spotting a possible hairline fracture in Baxter's back left leg.

Another pair of silver doors led into the ICU. I braced for the proliferation of medical equipment, the *beep-beep-beep* of lifesaving machines. But Baxter was the only ICU patient. And so, while there was a variety of medical paraphernalia throughout the room, some pieces covered in plastic, it was quiet. In the middle was a nurses' station where two women looked up at me and smiled.

Dr. Kasha walked me to the other side of the room, which resembled the back room of a groomer's or the nap room of a doggy day care. Various-sized kennels were stacked along the walls, stuffed animals and toys on a table in the middle.

"Baxter," I whispered.

He was in one of the larger crates along the left wall, asleep on a plush bed the color of sky.

"Can I touch him?"

"Sure, just avoid that leg."

Baxter woke up at the sound of our voices. He raised his head. His eyes were at half-mast, the way they get when something roused him but he was hoping he could go back to sleep soon.

But when he saw me, his eyes widened. *Yip.* This tiny sound came from him. I'd never heard it before. *Yip.* That second one nearly made me burst into tears. But Baxter always got anxious when I cried, so I just hurried to him. Dr. Kasha opened the crate and I sat cross-legged outside. Baxy crawled out, slowly, too slowly, maybe because of the IVs in both front legs.

He looked up, licked my chin a few times, then collapsed on my lap.

"I'll be back," the vet said.

I loved his weight on me; it made me think of all the times he crawled on me in bed. Occasionally, I'd nudge him away—*Baxy, go find your own spot.* Never again.

"I love you, Baxter," I said.

No response. His head lolled to the side on my leg, his eyes shut.

I leaned down, sniffed for the delicious scent of him, but it was gone, replaced by antiseptic and something darker, something streetlike.

He lay, in repose, across my lap. But I could feel his heart beating in his little chest.

"I love you, Baxter." He made a faint snoring sound and cocked his head back a little more, baring the soft yellow fur of his neck.

I'd been told by a therapist that one of the best things a parent could do for their child was to tell them you loved them. Over and over until they felt it.

The therapist and I had been discussing my parents. I'd told him how my parents were the most amazing couple, how in love they were. I'd talked about them for months. One day, he started asking me if I *felt* loved by them.

I was embarrassed, but I answered quickly, without thinking. *No.* Then I started to hedge. *Of course they do love me. Technically. I know that.* I explained about them, about their intensity for each other. *They do love me. They did say that.*

Well, as important as it is to say, the therapist had responded, *it's more important that the recipient feel it.*

"I love you, Baxter," I said, scooting myself back so I could lean forward and put my head near his chest, my mouth near his head. "I love you, Baxter. I love you."

24

"Okay, I think it's time for Baxter to get some sleep," someone said.

I straightened up. My back seized. How long had I been bent over Baxter like that?

I looked around, almost as if I were coming to, the way Baxter had. Still no one in the ICU but us and the nurses. And Dr. Kasha standing over us.

"He's asleep," I said. I looked back down at Baxter, who sighed and shifted around. "I think he's comfortable."

"He is," she said kindly. "But I'm really not supposed to have you back here for this long."

"Oh. Okay." I didn't move. None of us did. "What am I supposed to do now?"

"I'd suggest you go home and try to get some sleep. Do you have a car here?"

"I don't have a car," I said. Then I said, "Marilyn Miles." As if that explained everything. "I don't want to leave him."

"You're welcome to stay in the waiting room."

Silence. Finally, I said, "Okay."

Dr. Kasha and a nurse moved Baxter to the kennel, waking him up in the process. As the kennel doors closed, he seemed wide-awake suddenly. He tried to give his body one of his doggy shakes, but the movement could only reach his little shoulders before the pain, apparently, was too much. He seemed to freeze, black eyes unblinking.

"Baxter!" I said.

"He's okay," Dr. Kasha said. She reached in and petted him softly, and the gesture calmed him. He looked at me forlornly, his eyes asking, *What is happening and why did it happen?*

The walk down the hallway back to the waiting room went too fast. I pushed the silver doors, this time expecting the sterile, brown-sofa'd vacuum of the waiting room. But it was no longer empty.

"Dude, get over yourself."

Gavin?

He was leaning on the front desk in sort of a casual way, but his voice was tight, nearing loud.

He didn't see me right away, and the person he spoke to had their back to me. It was a man. Dark hair.

"Sebastian?"

Both of them turned, angry expressions on their faces.

"Jess," Sebastian said, his face clearing. He moved

to me, looking down from his six-two height. "Is he okay?" His eyes were anguished.

I shrugged. I shook my head. Then I started to cry. Sebastian pulled me to him, pulling my face into his T-shirt, into the smell of him, and I felt comfort rush over and around me, as if I'd been plunged into a bath of it. I hugged him back.

I allowed myself a few sobs, hugging Sebastian tighter than I had in a long, long time, before I registered Gavin's presence again.

I disentangled myself from Sebastian's embrace, which seemed reluctant then. "Hi," I said to Gavin. I hugged him then, too.

"Why didn't you call me?" Gavin said. His voice sounded pained.

"I couldn't remember your phone number. I didn't have my cell phone."

When I pulled away from Gavin's hug, I took a step back. And I realized I was standing there between the two of them, almost equidistant to each of them.

"How did you know?" I said to Gavin.

"I called every pet hospital in town. The news of Baxter getting hit has been all over the internet."

"Really?" I looked to Sebastian.

His expression registered embarrassment. "I don't know." He looked at Gavin then with what looked like scorn. "I don't watch stuff like that."

"Like I said, dude, get over yourself."

"'Dude, get over yourself'?" Sebastian said in a mocking tone. "Really?" His voice was getting louder.

"Uh, gentlemen," I heard. The receptionist stood, looking hesitant.

But Sebastian didn't break his gaze from Gavin's. "Dude," he said, with more scorn. "What are you, some kind of surfer? You want to follow that up with how you can ride a rad wave?"

"You think you're some hot shit?" Gavin's voice grew loud, too.

"Guys!" My word was a bark, as biting as Baxter's could be. "Guys," I said again.

I looked at Gavin. "Is there a video of Baxter getting hit?" I was horrified.

"No, but there's a shot of the SUV driving away." He shook his head, as if to say, *It doesn't matter.* "How is he?" Gavin said, his voice measured, as if falling back in time, away from the skirmish with my ex-husband.

"I don't know," I said. "I don't know."

25

A grueling night— Sebastian, Gavin and I all in the silent, sterile waiting room, all night.

Sebastian shot Gavin eye daggers, once suggesting aloud that Gavin could go home, but Gavin returned to the laid-back guy I knew and didn't take the bait. He sat near me, but not so close it would be uncomfortable for Sebastian. Every hour or so he ran to a convenience store down the street and bought snacks, drinks.

He'd also bought some magazines. "To distract us," he said. Then he sat right next to me, cutting off my view of Sebastian.

He flipped through a magazine, almost as if he was doing it for me, and I leaned on him, staring down at it, blankly noting a celeb wedding, some celeb's kid.

"Is this the magazine you work for?" I said when he opened another one.

"Yeah." He made a bitter-sounding laugh. "I can't

believe I actually put money back into it by buying these."

He often complained about his job. And I wanted anything right then to really distract me.

Sebastian had gotten up and was across the room on his cell phone. Who knew who he was talking to?

"What's so bad about your job?" I asked, my voice low.

It didn't take long for him to answer. "I sell nothing. I mean, I literally sell a blank space. Someone else will come up with the words or images that will go there. Someone else will design how those words and images will look on a screen. I do nothing of substance."

"Not everyone creates something. In fact it's kind of painful sometimes to be one of the people who do." I told him how my parents fretted over their work.

"But I always wanted to create," he said.

We heard a frustrated sound and both looked at Sebastian, who was looking at his phone. Then he was on it again, talking, moving farther away.

"He gets to create," Gavin said, looking at Sebastian. "I can't stand him, but I keep reading his stuff. He is really talented."

And we were back to my ex-husband and his job, which was a better topic than Baxter's health, but still a bummer.

Luckily, Dr. Kasha came out then.

"Nothing yet," she said. Again.

A few hours later, another vet, a guy. He essentially summarized everything he'd learned about Baxter's case, but he had no real info or updates.

But then finally, a few hours after dawn, the male vet stepped out, the double doors swing-swinging behind him. This time he cut his words short.

"He's going to be okay," the vet announced.

None of us moved.

"Baxter is going to be just fine," he said.

Sebastian dropped his head in his hands, murmuring, "Thank God. Thank God."

I covered my mouth with my hand, not sure I'd heard right, afraid to feel good. Gavin scooted closer and put his arm around my shoulders.

"The IV fluids addressed his BUN elevation," the vet said. "And the ortho saw him just now and there is no leg fracture. He was concerned about a pelvic avulsion but he ruled that out. The spot in the eye is reducing. He hasn't shown any other signs of concussion."

"Now what?" I asked.

He smiled. "Now you can take him home."

Home. My condo was filled with balloons and flowers and gift baskets and cards.

"I don't know who most of these people are," I said, putting down a Get Well Soon card that read,

"Superdog, we love you! Missy, Charlie and Lucky Chapman."

Another was on the letterhead of a lawyer from Chicago. She also wished Baxter well, then added, "Our dog, Bob, is a terrier. He usually only likes girl dogs, but my husband and I think he and Baxter would be friends." Their phone number followed. A photo had been included in the envelope. Bob was a short but very solid dog the color of sand, his snout nearly as big as his chest.

"I don't know any of them," Sebastian said, looking at some of the gifts. He had Baxter in a football hold against his chest. Baxter's head lay on his blue shirt, sleeping.

But then I saw one from Betsy, mother of the toddler who Baxter tackled on the video.

> *Dear Jessica,*
> *I hope you are both doing okay. I break into tears every time I think about Baxter being hit! Every night when I put Clara to sleep, I kiss her and we say good-night to God and then to Baxter.*
> *Love, Betsy.*

The card made me a little weepy, too. I looked at Baxter. *He'll doze a lot,* the vet had said when he discharged us. *He has mild soft tissue injuries. You'll want to keep him on the pain meds for a few days, but it will make him drowsy.*

The words *soft tissue injuries,* which would have slain me if Baxter had suffered them last week after, say, running too hard at the park, were now little uttered gifts. *That's all he has! Soft tissue injuries!* I kept hearing the slam of the SUV against Baxy's tiny body, but then I reminded myself, *That's all he has! Soft tissue injuries!*

But something else the vet said was nagging at me. He'd heard Sebastian and me discussing Baxter. We'd been talking about when we got Baxter, yet it must have been clear we were no longer together.

"So who does he live with?" the vet had said.

"We both have him," I said, my finger pointing to Sebastian, then myself.

The vet's brows came closer together. "So he goes back and forth?"

"Yeah. We have joint custody." Funny how that joint custody thing had seemed so adorable in the news piece. Now it sounded silly. "We share him," I said, which only made it worse.

"How does he handle that?" the vet said, his head nodding toward Baxter.

"Fine," Sebastian said with a snap in his voice.

But I was thinking about when we first got divorced. We'd both been miserable, heartbroken, and we'd both remarked that Baxter seemed to be suffering through his own grief.

When I'd first noticed his sluggishness during that time, I thought it was me being hyperaware. Or maybe Bax was unhappy without Sebastian. Sometimes I would open a closet door to find he had pulled from far-reaching hangers a sweater (or other garment of Sebastian's he hadn't yet moved) and made a bed of it. This from a dog who loved to sleep in the sun on the hardwood floor. We'd never known him to burrow into closets, Sebastian's clothes or no.

It made me want to cry—finding our sweet pup, a golden mass of curls, his round black eyes looking up at me as if to say, *This is all I can find of him.*

The first few times I made the mistake of saying, "Oh, Baxy. He's here. Sebastian is here."

I meant existentially he was still around, that he was still Baxy's dad, but just the words *He's here* sent Baxter bolting from the closet. He ran, frantically, from room to room, searching, yipping. The cries from that dog's throat felt like blades through me, mirroring my own.

"Baxy, Baxy," I said, running after him. "Come! Stay!" But you can't explain to a dog, *I just meant he's not "here" here. He's still alive—he's around.*

I thought about giving Sebastian full custody or at least giving him more time with the dog. I couldn't be selfish or let the dog be unhappy when he missed Sebastian so much.

But similar things happened at the corporate

apartment Sebastian rented those first few months, one I'd never set foot in, had no claim to.

"He finds anything that smells like you," Sebastian said, describing a similar episode of Baxy's at his place. "Once, he found something of yours in my pocket."

"What was it?" What piece of me had Sebastian been carrying around?

"Makeup. A compact."

I felt a tinge of disappointment. I'd thought, for a moment, that Sebastian had been purposely holding on to something, but he was only speaking of the backup, nearly gone powder I sometimes put in Sebastian's coat when we went out together and I didn't want to carry a purse.

"That MAC compact," Sebastian said. "The gold one." I would not have thought Sebastian would ever register that kind of information—the brand of makeup I used—or be able to describe it.

"Did he just want to chew on the case?" I said.

"No." Sebastian shook his head. "He hid it. Since then he's somehow smuggled other stuff of yours from your place and hidden it at mine."

"Like what?"

"One of your blue socks."

"The cashmere ones? I lost one of those a long time ago."

"I think he stuffed it in the hole in the side of that tennis ball."

"Are you serious?" I was smiling now. "That's so cute."

"He misses both of us, Jess," Sebastian said.

And the smile slid from my expression. I knew what he meant—he misses us *together*.

Eventually, Baxy got better, his spirit returned (although he still stole socks on occasion).

Still, the vet at the hospital hadn't been convinced.

"Have you guys heard about the Blue Star Dog Ranch?" he asked.

"The Blue Star Dog Ranch?" Sebastian said, not sounding impressed.

"It's like a dog ranch and spa." He caught Sebastian's expression. "Seriously, it's nicer than any hotel I've ever been to—totally lux—and the dogs can get spa treatments and physical therapy. A lot of people send their dogs there when they're out of town, but I know of a lot of dogs that went to recover from injuries or illness."

"Where is this place?" I asked.

"Somewhere in Wisconsin. Come with me." He took us into an office and pulled up Blue Star Dog Ranch on the computer.

The ranch was legit. Fenced-in fields and riding greens. A handsome row of white-roofed red barns. And a manor at the back of the property—sprawling, exquisitely decorated and exquisitely luxurious. Bear furs hung on the walls of the living room, the beamed ceiling above three stories high. Small pieces of furniture—resembling large, furry bean bags—were arranged around a roaring fire. In another photo the bean bags held dogs—an apricot poodle in one, a French bulldog next to a German shepherd in another.

"And this place is all for dogs," Sebastian said. He'd lost his cranky tone and now sounded almost wistful.

"Check it out," the vet said. He clicked on the welcome button and we watched a video of a chocolate Lab and his owners being greeted at the ranch. A receptionist gave the owners a beer and the Lab a packet of treats, a bone and a big bowl of water.

A movement brought me back to my living room. Now Sebastian was brushing the curly hair from Baxter's eyes and kissing the top of his head. I walked across the room to them. "Do you think he should go to that ranch?" I said.

"Do you?"

I thought about it. "No, I don't think he'd want to be away from us."

"Exactly," Sebastian said, ruffling the fur on Baxter's head.

He asked a question about medications. Soon we were talking softly, our heads bent over our sleeping dog. I didn't realize how close we were until Gavin cleared his throat. I'd almost forgotten he was there.

I leaned away. "I do think Baxter should be in only one of our places for a while," I said, raising the level of my voice a little and looking at Gavin as if to consult him, as well. "I think he should stay here."

"But I'm going away in a few days," Sebastian said.

"I know."

He looked at Baxter, his face sad. The dog leaned into Sebastian but could only seem to get so far, having none of his usual spring or sprite.

"I just think he should rest in one place," I said, trying to explain more. "He should have to adjust as little as possible."

"Yeah, you're right." Sebastian bounced his hip a little, as if gently bouncing an infant. He turned away and returned to appraising the gifts—stuffed animals and gift baskets filled with dog cookies.

I smiled at Gavin, who frowned, but I couldn't read him.

I picked up another card. I'd already read about eight florists' cards from names I didn't recognize, some addressed to Superdog, some to Baxter, some to Bax and myself.

A bouquet of white and yellow asiatic lilies was addressed to Sebastian Hess and Jessica Champlin. "We have joint custody, too!" the card said. "Thinking of you from Texas. Shannon Ritter and Malcom Went."

I glanced at Gavin who stood next to me, reading it. He shook his head a little and I could feel a rift between us, one apparently caused by my ex and the fact that we shared the dog.

I thought about what to say to him to make him feel better. I wanted to make this experience inclusive, if possible.

"Gav," I said. I took a perverse pleasure in the way Sebastian turned at the sound of that nickname. "Would you mind helping me keep track of the cards and addresses or emails if we have them? I want to write thank-you notes."

It was a bullshit task, and I think Gavin knew it. I think he was also grateful for it.

"Yeah, sure," he said, turning around, clapping his hands as if coming out of a huddle.

I picked up another card that showed a cartoon of two people boxing. When you opened the card, it read, "Never Give Up!"

There were a few lines written there. I skimmed them, then made myself stop and really read. "We've joined the hunt for the driver. We'll get them, whoever they are!"

"Hey," I said, turning, "this card says something about the hunt for the driver."

"Yeah," Gavin said. "Once the video of Baxter being hit went nuts, people kept commenting that they should find the driver and charge him with a hit-and-run."

"Really?" I said. "That's taking it a little far."

"Is it?" Gavin said. "He hit a dog and took off. He didn't even ask if it was okay."

"Why do you assume the driver's a he?" Sebastian said.

"I can't imagine a woman being that big of an asshole," Gavin said. He was looking directly at Sebastian when he spoke.

"He or she," I said, "doesn't matter. The accident was technically our fault. *My* fault. I shouldn't have let Bax carry that ball in his mouth, not when he was so attached to it he'd run out into the busy street to retrieve it."

"It wasn't your fault," Sebastian said.

"I just wish I could tell them to stop looking for the driver."

"Why?" Gavin said. "That driver should be caught and criminally charged. That's what people are saying, and people seem into the mystery of it."

"But Bax is going to be fine," I said. "And everyone has done something wrong before."

Sebastian glanced at me and held my gaze for a long moment, then looked away. Now it was his reaction I couldn't read.

"If the public thinks that driver should be caught and they can help, then let the public do the work it wants to do," Gavin said, sounding very sure about his opinion.

"What if the only thing the public wants is revenge for revenge's sake?" Sebastian asked Gavin.

"Who cares?" he answered.

"Well, I care about people being accused rightfully," Sebastian said.

"It doesn't sound like you care much about your dog."

That caused Sebastian to swallow hard, like he did when he wanted to quash an emotion. "It doesn't sound like you know much about anything."

Gavin's mouth was tense. He pulled out his phone, his thumb scrolling. "I don't think you could stop this if you wanted to."

He took a few steps toward me, holding it out for me to see. "Just watch this, Jess. They've got someone analyzing a video of the license plate."

"Are you serious?" Sebastian said, moving closer, looking at the phone, then pulling his own from his pocket.

On Gavin's phone I saw the car that had hit Baxter. The accident must have been caught by a video camera on some building across the street. It showed the car screeching away, then showed it again and again, each repetition of the video adding to a collection of results at the bottom, seeming to be getting closer to an identification of the license plate.

"It's an Illinois license," Gavin said, glancing from his phone to me, acting as if Sebastian wasn't there. "Starts with *H-7-Y.* They got it on an angle, so they haven't figured out the last part of it."

Sebastian muttered something.

"And see all these posts?" Gavin said. I read the one he had pulled up. It was written by a law student, commenting on the video, saying she'd done research and believed that the driver who "brazenly mowed down Superdog" could be charged with either leaving the scene of an accident or cruelty to a dog, a Class 4 felony, holding the potential of one to three years in prison.

"This is crazy," I said.

I felt terrible suddenly, even worse than I'd felt looking down at Baxter in the ICU. It was my fault that the accident had happened. If I'd been more responsible, I wouldn't have let Baxter carry the ball on the street. And as always, I felt immense compassion for someone who had done something stupid and who ran the risk of getting in big, big trouble for it. I knew that situation well.

"They're out for blood," Gavin said.

26

Three days later, Toni called me. "They got him."

"They got who?" I said.

I was in the kitchen with Baxter, trying to coax him into taking a pain med that I'd hidden in a cube of cheese. But he only chewed the cheese and spit out the tablet that I'd broken in half. Then he slumped onto the kitchen floor, crossing his paws in front of him, putting his chin on them, looking up at me and lifting one eyebrow, as if to say, *Are you kidding me, sister?*

"The SUV driver," Toni said. "He's a big dude, too."

"Oh," I said, not processing too much. "C'mon, Bax," I said, stuffing a halved pill in another cube of cheese and nudging it toward him.

He sniffed and turned his head aside as if in grand distaste.

"Let's go," I said. "Don't make me put this thing down your throat."

"What?" Toni said.

"I'm talking to Baxter. He can sniff out medication like a bomb dog does a grenade."

Baxter nudged his snout in his paws and covered his eyes.

"So they have him at the station," Toni said.

"The driver. At a police station?"

"Yeah! He was arrested."

"Oh, God." I felt terrible for the guy. Yes, he'd hit a dog who ran into the road, but he couldn't have predicted it. He couldn't have predicted his instinct to run. And like I'd told Gavin many times now, it was my fault for not supervising Baxy better.

Sebastian quietly agreed with my stand on the issue of the driver. He was around much of the weekend while Baxter slept and slept and slept. Gavin was great, running any errands I needed, looking things up on the internet about dog health. But when the topic turned to the driver, all I heard from Gavin was a chorus of things like, *What an asshole!* and *Freaking coward* and *They need to send him away.*

I knew he was just feeling protective of me and Baxter. And I hated that I couldn't tell him why I felt so strongly about it—about people making mistakes in life and still getting another shot. I'd never spoken about my life with Billy McGowan to anyone. I'd been there for the beginning of the McGowan Brothers' fame but by the time they were superstars, no one remembered the girl Billy had been married to. And I didn't want to remember or talk about it. It was a life that was dead.

"They want to know if you want to give a statement outside the police station," Toni said.

"No!"

"That's what I said." Toni hadn't told me whether she agreed with me or not about the driver but she'd heard my side. "They still want you to come in, though. Even if you're not making a statement. I can probably get out of here in a few hours and go with you."

I swallowed hard. I hadn't been to a police station since my arrest.

"Jess?" Toni said. "You there?"

"Yeah, yeah."

I reminded myself that since I was in a new life, and since that old life was dead, I would go to the station and do what I had to. And that was that. No fear.

"Sebastian is due here any minute." I said, "to spend some time with Baxy. It might be nice for him if they had boy time."

Baxter perked up at the mention of Sebastian's name. Then he looked tired again and dropped his head. His nose was now about an inch from the tablet he'd spit out of the cheese again. He sniffed it a few times, then stared at it drowsily.

"Want me to meet you there?" Toni said.

"I'm going to go now and get it over with. I think

I can handle it myself." I settled Baxter onto his dog bed in my room. "I'll call you if I need you."

Then I left a key and a note for Sebastian at the front desk, and left the building.

"I don't want to press charges."

"It's not your choice, ma'am." The state's attorney, a young guy with surprisingly white-gray hair, had said this more than once. Zack Nelson was his name. He'd given me his card after I'd talked to a detective. He'd then taken me into another room, one a bit bigger and nicer than the cement room I'd been in with the cop.

"But I'm the victim, right? Or my dog was."

"You were both victims. But it remains up to the state to determine if charges are pressed. And we determine yes."

"Who's 'we'?"

"The State's Attorney's Office determines charges," he said. The guy had no expression on his face.

"Don't I have some say in this?"

"Not really."

"Not really?" I repeated.

"We have sole discretion."

I looked at the fake wood table and thought about calling Gavin, someone from my new life, for support. But I knew he'd want to tell Zack Nelson to throw in more charges and send the guy to prison.

I looked back up.

"Ms. Champlin?" he said, in a "will that be it?" kind of way.

"I want to meet him. What's his name… Gary Stips."

Finally, the guy's face moved. In fact, his eyebrows rose. "Oh, no," he said. "We could never let you meet with him alone."

"I didn't say I needed to be alone."

He hesitated, and I knew in that moment he had discretion on this, too. I kept flashing back to myself in the police station, that awful time.

I stood. "Let's go."

27

I had never seen a man cry like that—with heaving abandon and grief. And now, in an interrogation room with someone crying, I couldn't help but re-feel my own time in such a room.

Emotions swung through me as if running a test of every single one I could experience. I felt flushed, then exhausted, then beyond anxious. That event in my past had been so jarring, so visceral, a sawing away of everything and everyone I'd known.

Gary Stips, this man in front of me now, tried to bat his tears away with the back of one fist while his other was handcuffed to a wall.

He was mad, too. Mad at himself. "I'm such a fuckup. That's what I was thinking when I was driving around that day. That I'd fucked up something else. And then *wham!* I hit your dog."

More flashbacks now, but those of the accident. Suddenly, I wanted, needed, out of there as fast as possible. I looked at Zack Nelson, who stood in the corner. He shrugged, like, *You wanted this*.

"You know what?" I leaned across the desk, toward the driver. "Gary, listen to me. The dog is fine. He is. Not one broken bone."

"That's what you said."

"It's true."

"Thank God." He looked right at me then, tears still falling. "You also said he was sleeping a lot. Why?"

"He has soft tissue injuries, and they've given him pain meds. The combination makes him drowsy."

"I saw somewhere on the internet he can't run. For how long?"

"Another ten days."

More crying. "You should never forgive me."

"Gary, I've already forgiven you. And that's why I don't want charges pressed."

I looked at Zack Nelson, most bored man on the planet. He may have been playing a game of chess in his head, because he did not seem intellectually present right then.

"Mr. Nelson," I said. "I'd like to officially request that no charges be filed against Gary."

Nelson gave me a military-style nod. "Your request will be noted for… Oh, for no one. Request denied." He opened the door and said something to an officer in the hall.

Nelson came back in the room and closed the

door. "You're already too late. Charges are done. He'll be transported to lockup shortly."

I looked at Gary Stips. He was stricken. I remember that feeling. My gut clenched for the man. And for the Jessica of yesteryear.

"I'm going to work on this," I said to Gary.

Without addressing Nelson, I stood and strode past him, thinking fast. I went out in front of the station. It faced a multilaned street, but it was a lonely area. An area of town no one called home.

I pulled out my phone and called Toni. She answered on the first ring. "Tell me."

"I do need some help after all. I think I should make a statement."

"Hold on," she said. "Let's talk this through."

I related my meeting with the detective, then the state's attorney, then Gary Stips. I told her how the state's attorney had refused to consider my request to not press charges.

"Well, it's good you asked a couple of times," Toni said. "Even if the guy was an asshole about it. Because you can use that with the press if we have to, you know, make it sound like official requests were made."

"And I really did get a ruling from that jackass. Denied."

"Hmm. Question—did your dogwear orders go up after Baxter was hit?"

"Yes." There was no denying the numbers.

"And did they go up again when people started looking for the driver?"

"Yes. And we got a lot more followers." We'd received emails and messages on social media from all over the world. *We're thinking of you, Superdog! We'll wear our collars in solidarity.*

"Okay, then," Toni said, sounding excited.

"I see where you're going with this. You think I can have a similar result with a press conference."

"Yes. With your dog in your arms, imploring the police to let the guy go."

"That's a bit much," I said.

"Sounds like it's going to take much to get that Gary guy out of there."

"Hold on a sec." I put my cell phone on speaker and looked at the call log. "I've been getting calls from the plant in Grand Rapids for the last few hours."

"You want to check in with them?"

"Yeah. I'll call you right back."

The phone rang for a long time in Grand Rapids before a harried-sounding woman's voice answered. I identified myself and asked for the manager on my product.

"Oh, my gosh," the woman said. "He'll really want to talk to you."

In a few seconds he was on the phone, his words coming fast about how orders for my products had been coming directly to their plant. "I don't know how they tracked us down!" he said. "We've never had this happen, but over the last few days, it's gone nuts. We're running full steam."

"Amazing," I said. "What do you need from me?"

"We hired a few people, so you just keep going!"

I called Toni back. "Okay, our timing is spooky. The orders are coming to them directly now. Looks like more attention around the accident could really keep biz great. But I don't want to do a press conference just for that. Mostly, I want to implore them not to charge the guy. I want them to leave him alone. I want him to be able to put this behind him."

I didn't add, *Like I've put my past behind me.*

"I'll put the word out to the media," Toni said.

"I should call Gavin and Sebastian. Then I'll get Baxter. The dogger will be psyched. He's been getting bored at home. Meet you here in an hour?"

"See you then."

28

I called Gavin and practically beseeched him as my boyfriend to support me on the decision to call a press conference.

"I can't believe you're doing so much for this guy."

I told him how in addition to wanting to do it, giving a public statement would also be good for I'd Rather Sleep with the Dog.

"Well, at least there's that," he said.

I told him how Gary Stips had been sobbing in the interrogation room. "He's been punished enough," I said.

Gavin climbed on board, grudgingly, agreeing to support me in not wanting to press charges. Once he'd decided that, he was amazing, saying that of course he'd be at the press conference.

I closed my eyes as I hung up the phone with him, letting the appreciation for him, for us, run through me.

I called Sebastian then, and he, too, said I should do the press conference if it could help my business.

"And, Jess," he said. "I do completely understand your opinion that everyone deserves a second chance from their mistakes. I completely agree with you."

My appreciation soared.

But then I asked if he would be at the press conference.

"No."

"That was a fast answer."

"I can't, Jess. I really can't. The one news piece I did was it. If I keep doing these things, my name will get out there."

"Wouldn't that help you in some way?" I asked. "Get you more readers?"

"I doubt it."

"But this *is* news," I said resignedly.

"Sorry, Jess," he said. "I can't."

"You won't."

He didn't answer.

Two hours after I'd called Toni we were in front of the station. In that short amount of time, Toni had worked magic. News trucks for four local stations and two national networks were lined up under streetlamps. Reporters stood around consulting with cameramen under supplemental lights. Toni had also gotten two radio stations, four print magazines, six photographers and some bloggers.

Toni put me at the podium with Baxter, who

awoke occasionally to give a big pink-tongued yawn, which the photogs snapped. Gavin was behind me.

"So just so you know," Toni said. "They're going to have their say after you do." She explained that standing on the other side of the set, waiting to comment on my statement, were the arresting officer, the detective and the state's attorney.

"I figured," I said. I had caught Zack Nelson just a moment ago, crouching in front of a squad car's mirror, trying to fix his hair with his fingers.

When the lights were all on, I had to blink profusely to try and clear my vision. I held Baxter closer to me. He squeezed his eyes shut against the brightness.

I read my statement, asking again that the Cook County State's Attorney's Office accept my request. I said that since there was no harm to person or property (or dog), the charges against Gary Stips should be dropped.

When I was done, Zack Nelson stepped forward and spoke into the mic. "If we were to allow people to run over our pets and take off, never even asking if the pet is okay, what kind of society would that make us?"

A hand shot up from the CBS reporter. "Do we have a particularly big problem in Cook County with dog hit-and-runs?"

Zack looked confused by the question, then sighed and answered, "Well, not exactly. But this is the kind of thing we like to get on top of. You don't want to set a precedent."

"How much will it cost to prosecute Mr. Stips?" another reporter asked. They didn't seem to have faith in Zack coming up with anything original to say.

"I'd have to do the math…."

Everyone silent. *Okay, we'll wait for that math.*

"I think it's like twenty-five grand," the first reporter said to the second.

"More, if someone is in custody," another added.

Zack murmured something about the job of a state's attorney. The press had completely lost interest and were looking back to me.

I looked at Toni with a question in my eyes. She gave me a nod.

"I have one more thing to add," I said, stepping toward the mic again, holding up my phone. "Actually, I just have something to show you. A video. Baxter met Mr. Stips tonight." I hit Play and showed the clip of Baxter in a white interrogation room with Gary Stips. Baxter licked Stips's tears, who laughed lightly when Bax kept it up.

"Excuse me!" Zack said. "Pets are not allowed in the station."

He looked around for who might have been responsible. The detective who'd told me he thought Zack Nelson had "a stick up his ass" raised his hand and waved it toward Zack as if to say, *Let it go.*

A reporter asked me why I was "so keen" on having the charges dropped against Mr. Stips.

"Because everyone makes mistakes," I said. "And everyone should be able to move on."

29

It was ten o'clock at night by the time the press conference was over. Within the hour, it ran on a local twenty-four-hour news station. Toni put that video on the internet, along with the one of Bax and Gary. People flooded both videos with comments. Many of the comments were supportive—talking about the power of apology and forgiveness, and how the world would be a better place if there was more in it. But a lot of people said I was a coward, that Gary Stips was a coward and that any man who would hit a dog and drive away should be hung. Essentially.

The controversy over what should be done drove the news stations and morning shows to air the story the next day and even run it a few times. Then all their websites were flooded with comments, too. The questions about punishment and forgiveness were discussed on morning shows and even debated at schools. A few days went by and more and more steam grew on the forgiveness side of things. *#Forgivness* and *#Superdog* were trending all the time.

A few days after that, the State's Attorney's Office issued a one-sentence statement. "Our office will be dropping all charges against Gary Stips."

The morning after that, my website crashed.

Too many orders, too much activity. Like the plant in Grand Rapids, I had to suddenly (and without great thought) hire people to pitch in—on the web side, the design side and the order side.

Sebastian left for another trip. It barely entered my mind that I did not know where he was, would never know those things about him, about his work. I was strangely okay with it. Something about advocating for Gary Stips and giving him a chance to move on reminded me that I had done the same, gave me that alive feeling again. Any remaining issues with Sebastian also hurt less because I had Gavin, and because I had Baxter.

Baxy was doing okay. Surprisingly okay for a fifteen-pound scrap of fluff (albeit a tenacious, adorable one) who had survived such a blow. But he wasn't unscathed. He flinched on the street when a car was too close. And he seemed to keep finding himself off balance.

It was the balance thing that really troubled me. I only allowed him the ball now when we were in the park, far from traffic. When we finally got there, and I held the ball, he would shake his tail and dip his chest to the ground, miming, *Let's go, let's go. Throw the thing.* And every time I did he responded like he always did—a sprint in the direction of the ball. If the ball merely skidded instead of bouncing, all was good. Bax would snag it in his teeth and run it back to me.

But when the ball had any kind of a bounce, that's where he hit an issue. He'd leap onto his back paws, crane his neck and snap his jaws, as usual, but every time that week, he'd miss it by an inch or sometimes even a few.

It sounded small, but it didn't feel small for a dog with Baxter's ball mastery. Fortunately and much to my relief, every day, the balance got better, he got closer and closer to catching the ball, and eventually he started to catch again.

It was Gavin's easy presence that saved us both during that time.

Gavin left work early every day and he helped me answer phones, work with the new people, lug shipments in and out of the studio. I kept telling him he shouldn't jeopardize his job.

He scoffed. "You can't jeopardize something that's not worth valuing."

In fact, Gavin helped me out with any little thing until eight or nine at night when we would walk the few blocks to my place. If it was late, he carried Baxter in a football hold under his arm. I'd never seen him do that until after Sebastian had, and I wondered if the mimic was intentional. Either way, I liked seeing the guy I was falling in love with holding my dog-kid close to his chest, murmuring in his ear.

When we got home at night, Baxter would sleep on one of the dog beds we now had in each room. Gavin would put candles on the kitchen table, every day, making the glass in the bay window sparkle. Sebastian and I had never thought to do something like that.

If we didn't order out food, we cooked, together, making something out of the scraps in my fridge. Sebastian used to cook for me. Gavin and I did it together. Although maybe I shouldn't call it cooking, since it was mostly combining foods and nuking them, but we had fun doing it. Sex in the kitchen became a not-so-uncommon thing, me sitting on the island, my legs stretched across to the other counter, Gavin holding up the rest of my weight.

In the mornings, sometimes Gavin would catch me when I was getting out of bed and pull me back He would whisper something low, then start to stroke some part of my skin.

"You like that?" he would say, not in a sexual way exactly, but as if simply out of curiosity, wanting to figure out which parts of my skin were more sensitive to his touch.

"Mmm," I said, usually too relaxed to form words.

Back and forth, his touch went over my skin. With each brush, I began to feel lulled, as if I were floating. With each brush, he was sweeping me lighter, sweeping me clean.

His soft touch would move to my shoulders, my arm, my forearm. He turned my hand over and stroked my palm.

Such great mornings.

During those weeks, my decision to stay in Chicago after the divorce made even more sense. *Ah!* I thought. This *is why I'm still here.*

Moving to Chicago had been rocky at the start. First, there was my business as a stylist, which was much harder to grow than I thought. Chicago is streakier than New York. People, wisely, pull back the purse strings when they're sensing difficult times ahead, when the threat of an Antarcticlike winter looms, when it's too hot to think of wearing anything other than "something that won't show sweat" like it had been that August.

Moving to Chicago had also been challenging on the personal front with the dawning realization that, before me, Sebastian had slept with seemingly every hot, smart girl in Chicago.

Back then we ate out a lot, and that's when it often happened—the discovery that we'd run into yet another ex of some sort. We might be leaving a restaurant, like, say, RL. Outside, a stunning redhead with great shoes and a seriously expensive briefcase. This was not only a hot woman, but a hot, smart woman who worked her ass off and did it well. You could just tell. That's what part of my job entailed—being able to intuitively take in everything about a client—their physical appearance, sure, but also their clothes, their attitude, the way they carried their shoulders, the squint or curious wideness of their eyes.

I would then see the adoring cast on the redhead's face when she saw Sebastian, then stood and waved. And I would see the disappointment when she registered me at his side, saw that he was holding my hand.

I remember a St. Patrick's Day when we were still living in New York but visiting Chicago in search of a condo, when we ran into not one but *three* people he'd been involved with. St. Patrick's Day, I had quickly learned, is like high holy day for Chicagoans. I'd lived in New York for a long time, so I'd seen people who knew how to party. And hell, I lived on the road with the McGowan Brothers Band for almost a year. But no one, *no one,* knows how to have a good time like Chicagoans on St. Paddy's Day.

Other than his mother, at whose place we were staying while in town, no one knew Sebastian and I were visiting. That's how he wanted it, he told me. "You and me in Chicago, me and you. This is how it's going to be here." He believed it when he said it. I know that. I believed him.

So we made our own pub crawl that St. Patrick's Day, walking south down Lincoln, barhopping all the way to Old Town.

We stopped at a place called Rose's for a few rounds of pool. "Take it easy, Jess," Sebastian said, smiling, eyeing me making fast headway through my beer while he chalked a cue stick. "We have to pace ourselves."

"What a surprise," we heard. A woman's voice. A very pretty dark-haired girl turned around in her bar stool. "I've never known you to pace yourself."

He said her name and introduced me. We played only one round of pool.

Next, we went to Irish Eyes, then John Barleycorn. I'd thought I'd gotten the Sebastian ex run-in out of the way. But then we went to a place called Four Farthings where Sebastian saw a woman who used to work at the same newspaper he did in New York. From there it was on to Bricks, a little hole in the ground led into by a bricked stairway and lights inside with red and gold tones.

We were having so much fun, kissing so much over our table in between occasional bites of pizza, that I never wanted to leave. But then a couple came in and the woman and Sebastian greeted each other in that awkward "wow, I didn't expect to see you" kind of way.

"We're going now. Good to see you," Sebastian said, pulling me outside. I tried to be mad, but maybe I was buzzed enough because it was funny. By the time we got outside, laughing, it seemed every single person in the city had hit the streets, as well. I'd never witnessed such a sight.

It was a strangely balmy day, and music poured from each window, each bar. Everyone was in high spirits, calling hello, slapping high fives with strangers on the street. There was a fair amount of stumbling and lots of people with arms around each other, apparently as much for support as for the camaraderie.

"So that was..." Sebastian said.

"That was awkward again. How many more, Hess?"

"Hey, you got to remember that other than New York, I've lived in this town for my whole life." He gave a sheepish grin. "They're all good women."

"I will admit, they all seemed very cool. And very pretty."

"And you're the prettiest and coolest of all." He kissed me.

With Gavin it was different thus far. No ex-girlfriend run-ins. Either Gavin hadn't had such a storied history or he didn't draw the same continued adoration after leaving relationships. Myself, though, I couldn't imagine not adoring him.

30

One night, Gavin and I were at my studio, finishing things up. He was whistling while he taped a few boxes of orders I still handled in-house.

"You are always so cheerful at the end of a workday," I said.

He stopped whistling, looked at me and smiled. "Am I?"

"Yeah, and I always feel cranky."

"This is just so much better than my job. It's so much more fulfilling."

He got a call then. He waved at me and took it out in the hallway.

I decided to tidy some of the stuff in the studio— bobbins of leather, boxes of embellishments (and clips and leads), and more boxes of sample materials.

When Gavin returned, it was as if someone else had walked in the room for him. His face had a definitely unhappy cast.

"What is it?" I asked.

"Work," he said.

"Oh, honey." I crossed the room and kissed him on the cheek. "Let's get out of here."

Gavin was nearly silent for much of the walk home, and pensive when we got there. He took another call and went to bed early. I didn't think too much of it. I felt bad that his job brought him down so much.

The next day would mark three weeks since my press conference. *Three great weeks.* That's how I would later think of that time—working insane hours, with Gavin at my side, and loving it.

In the morning, our plan was to sit outside somewhere with Baxter and have an egg-laden brunch and take some time off to breathe. Or at least I had suggested that. Gavin just assented.

As we walked, I tried to engage him in topics far away from either of our jobs. Gavin didn't perk up much. He tightly held one of my hands in his; the other held Baxy's leash.

I motioned for the leash, thinking that I should try to take any burdens off him, even something small like carrying the dog leash. "Want me to?"

"No," he said quickly.

To anyone who glanced our way, we must have looked a cohesive unit, a contented couple with a dog. But we didn't feel like a couple right then. Gavin seemed far away. He kept tsk-ing, as if gravely disappointed in something. Or someone.

"What's wrong?" I asked.

It took him a while to hear, or register, and then he shot a glance at me and shook his head, as if to say he didn't want to talk about it. He sighed.

"Seriously," I said, "did I piss you off?"

Shook his head again.

"What happened with that phone call last night?"

He stopped and looked at me fast. His face looked pained.

But then he slipped a strong arm around my lower back and pulled me to him, and right to his mouth. He kissed me for a long time. As we always had, we started to pull back from our kiss at the same time. I was about to suggest turning around, maybe picking something up from a market and eating breakfast in bed at my place. After.

But his embrace disappeared. I felt the relative cool of the air in its absence.

Gavin looked down at Baxter. "Sit, please," he said. I always thought it so cute that he said "please" and "thank you" to Baxter after giving a command.

Baxter sat and looked up at Gavin, then me, expectant of what was next, but ready to wait. He was used to taking commands from Gavin now, as well as Sebastian and me. In Gavin I'd found someone who adored me, was around all the time *and* loved my dog.

Then Gavin returned his eyes to me. "I have to talk to you about something. About something I did."

His words were vague. Yet they were so swift, they cut through the air, and drove right through me, like a sharp blade through paper.

"What? What is it?"

Gavin kept shaking his head. I couldn't see his eyes, hidden under the deep reflective bronze of his sunglasses.

"C'mon," I said, nudging Gavin.

He nodded and pointed to a nearby stoop. We sat and Baxter settled onto the pavement.

When he finally spoke, he said, very resignedly, "I found something out."

"Something?"

"About you."

"About me?"

"You and Billy McGowan," Gavin said. And he said it just like that—matter-of-fact.

I felt another zing through me.

Gavin took off his sunglasses, and his brown eyes—suddenly visible, vivid—mesmerized me, but I couldn't let myself get sucked into that gaze.

"What do you know about Billy?" I spoke plainly, with no intonation, no confirmation.

"You were married to him."

Now I paused. My parents knew about Billy and me getting married, and of course Billy's family knew. It was during the last year of us, when he denied cheating on me and wanted to show me how much he loved me. I lapped it up. I wanted us to be like my parents. But no one else knew, and when articles or books about the band came out, if I was mentioned at all it was always just "Billy's high school girlfriend."

"Yes," I said to Gavin. "We were married."

And it didn't feel bad, that admittance, that disclosure.

"And I know about your arrest," Gavin said.

The shadow of my past behind me grew darker. Shame swelled. Shame that had a muddy consistency to it, one that was hard to feel around or see through.

Baxter moved and sat on my feet, then lay down, as if he could sense the swell was trying to hold me there.

"Hey," Gavin said, reaching for my hand.

I jerked my hand away.

"That kind of shit happens to everyone," he said.

"What kind of shit is that?" I didn't want to admit anything. My father had paid a Manhattan attorney to expunge my record so that indications of my arrest could not be found. But I recall vividly the attorney warning us, *You can't hide anything forever.*

"Drug possession," Gavin said. "With intent to sell."

"*That's* the kind of shit that happens to everyone?"

He shrugged with one shoulder.

So. It had been found. By my boyfriend.

"How?" I said.

Why did he look confused? "How…?" he said.

"How did you find out. *Why?*"

"Superdog!" A woman's voice on the other side of me now. She was already bending down toward Bax who leaped to standing, ready to greet his public.

"We *love* him!" the woman said. She had ultra-tanned skin. "We watch him all the time!"

"Oh, great." My voice was weak.

Thirty seconds later, probably noticing that Gavin and I weren't talking, she moved on.

I looked at Gavin, whose face was a mask of agony. For himself? For me?

"Okay, so you know," I said. "And you said that *you* found it?"

"Yes."

"You, personally."

"Yes."

Anger flared. "Why were you looking up stuff on me?"

There was a long pause. Then he sighed. "Research."

"Research? For what?"

"I was trying to see if I could do it—you know, work on an actual story. It was you who encouraged me to try something on the editorial side."

My heart sank as I remembered all the times he'd talked about Sebastian's work. And how he wanted to do more than sell ads. And he was right, I'd encouraged him to try.

"So…" I said.

He pursed his lips together, apparently unable to speak.

"So you found this information about me," I prompted.

No response.

"You didn't tell them," I said, something dawning.

Slowly, he nodded. "I gave it to the magazine."

"The magazine you work for."

"Yes."

"No."

He gulped. "Not right away. Of course not."

"Of course," I said caustically.

"Seriously. I wasn't going to do anything about it, but then I saw you and Sebastian together when Bax got hit. I saw you still had a connection."

"Then you're the only one who sees it. And why did that make you want to give them the story?"

"Sebastian doesn't know, does he? About your arrest."

"No. Hardly anyone knows."

"Yeah. That's what I figured. So I thought that when Sebastian saw the story, it would only ensure you wouldn't get back together."

"And you? What did you think would happen with me and you?"

"There's nothing they could print that would make me think less of you."

I gave a bitter laugh, but his words registered.

"Print," I repeated. "Please tell me they're not going to run it."

He nodded. "They are. They love the story. That was the phone call I got last night."

"The story," I repeated.

"You know, Superdog's mom and all that."

"Oh, my God."

"I am so sorry."

"Are you?"

My mind whirled. I couldn't make sense of it. Or, as I realized later, maybe I didn't want to make sense of it. I was trying to hold all the memories of Billy and my arrest at bay, all my past. And I was very much not trying to think of my future, the one that involved being exposed in a celeb magazine.

Maybe it had to happen, maybe my past had to roar into my present. But I found I could not go lightly into that new future. It was as if I were holding back a screeching train, all by myself, using all the power of my body, or in this case my mind, to stop, stop, stop it from coming into my present.

"They have your mug shot," Gavin said.

The train couldn't be stopped. It plowed into and then through any thoughts, defenses, holdups in its path.

I got a flash of an image, the one that I hadn't seen since the year or two after my arrest when I ached from missing Billy, and even more, I bled from missing the "Billy and me" that I had fallen in love with.

I had smiled during my mug shot. I had never even partaken in cocaine, and for some reason, that made me feel less liable in my mind when I agreed to pick up coke for the band. Not once had I used drugs, although many were available on the road, especially when the McGowans' parents left the tour and returned to their businesses and their home. For some reason, I thought it helped that I wasn't a drug user, even a little bit. I was simply accepting a package.

When I was questioned, the police tried to get me to divulge the roles of each of the McGowans and how they were involved. I marshalled my strength like never before, and didn't mention anyone in the band. I wouldn't. Their reputation—meaning Billy's—could be tarnished. Granted, Billy's sparkle, in my mind, had been growing rusty since he had started using coke with regularity (and then hiding it when I commented on it). But despite that, despite his other transgressions, his betrayals, I still loved him deeply.

And so for me, but mostly for Billy and Billy and me, in case my arrest was revealed, I didn't want to take one of those horrible female mug shots. His brothers had dated girls who'd been arrested—open liquor charges and assault after a concert brawl—and inevitably the mug shots were horrible—hair askew, eyes too wide or too slitted, makeup dripping like black candle wax. Sometimes they would hit the papers or magazines, side by side with a photo of Mick singing to an adoring crowd. And I knew what happened to those girls after. Nothing. They were no longer part of the McGowan clan.

I was unlike those girls. I was more a member of the McGowan family than my own. Billy and I had been dating since we were fourteen. I felt a responsibility to uphold what they had worked for.

And so I had smiled.

Ultimately, it didn't matter because Billy ended it with me. Right then. He didn't even try to help in any way, nor did anyone from the band or the staff. And so the photo had never hit the newspapers. By the time the McGowan Brothers reached crazy fame, no one knew who I was or cared.

"When is this article coming out?" I asked now.

In the silence that followed, Gavin's face came into clearer focus.

Finally he spoke. "It went online last night. It started hitting the newsstands today."

Baxter made a slight whimpering noise, and I looked down. He was sitting at my feet, eyes up to me, head cocked to one side.

Thank God for you, I thought. *Thank God I have you.*

I looked back up and I studied Gavin's eyes. I crawled into them. I didn't hear him talking, although I vaguely noticed his mouth moving, the words *sorry* and *apologize* floated around. I wasn't really registering Baxter settling back in below me, then getting up a beat later when someone said, *Superdog!* Although I was somehow aware of that, too.

I knew enough to know that moment was precious—that moment before a whole life changes, again.

31

I left Gavin in a shocked state, my mind reeling from the fact that my arrest would be revealed, and worse, it would be revealed in a rather big way. I tried to remember the readership of the magazine Gavin worked for. One million people? Two? But I had rarely read it and never worked with them. I shook my head and picked up the pace. I marched down State Street, my destination suddenly clear. Baxter trotted alongside me, closer than usual, looking up at me every few seconds.

I can't believe him! Tears erupted in my eyes. *How could he do this?*

Before I'd left him, Gavin had said *I love you. I love everything about you.*

Words I'd always yearned to hear. And yet. And yet it was the end. And possibly the end of my new life. Who knew how an arrest record could affect I'd Rather Sleep with the Dog. Was it all coming to an end? I had to see the magazine, and how bad it was.

I bent down now on State Street and scooped Baxter up, putting him in a football hold the way Sebastian and Gavin did.

As I passed the corner of Oak and State, the pharmacy came into view. I put Baxter down again and walked faster.

I thought of Sebastian. Gavin was right that I'd never told him about my past. What would happen when he learned about the arrest and my other marriage? He would lose respect for me. That's the answer that kept coming into my mind. I tried to assuage myself with the fact that I'd lied to him via omission. I'd never mentioned the arrest or my marriage, and he hadn't asked. But I hadn't told him, either.

I finally reached the pharmacy. I tied up Baxter and walked, fast, into the store. *Where are the magazines? Where are the magazines?* I wasn't even sure if I was talking out loud or only in my head.

I found some. But only beauty and fashion. *Where are the rest? The tabloid ones?* I turned another corner and found what I was looking for—a hefty selection of magazines, including the one that employed Gavin, my boyfriend, my former boyfriend.

My eyes zeroed in on a yellow bubble at the top right of the magazine cover, one with red lettering.

It was almost as if I didn't want to read it, because

my eyes swam. But eventually they focused right on that yellow bubble.

Superdog Mom's Troubling Past

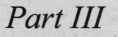

Part III

32

I stood with that magazine outside the pharmacy. I looked both ways, up State Street then toward my place. But even though the condo was only a few blocks away I couldn't go there. If I went home, then it would settle in, my rage and my grand disappointment would surge and overtake me. "It" was all too much already.

My phone rang again, as it had twice when I was in the pharmacy. I pulled it out of my purse. *Gavin.*

I hit the reject-with-message button and stuffed the phone to the bottom of my purse.

I crouched down by Baxter, kissing him on the top of his head, breathing in the warm doggy scent of him. Then I stood, flipped to page twenty-seven and made myself read the first sentence of the article.

"Superdog's mom is not as sweet as she pretends," it read.

And there was my mug shot. At least I had a grin on.

There was no byline, but I thought about the fact that Gavin might have edited the article, seen it in draft form or even written it. Which made the hurt so much worse, like a deep, squeezing vise on my chest.

I started reading the article, but my vision was jumpy. From what I could tell, the piece was short and accusatory, like many articles I'd seen in magazines like this. The wrath had just never been aimed at me before.

I made myself start at the beginning. Jessica Champlin, the article said, was "a child bride" to rockstar Billy McGowan. As if Billy hadn't been eighteen right along with me. As if we hadn't decided to spend our lives together.

I remembered suddenly when Billy told me he wasn't going to college. We were seniors in high school then.

"What do you mean?" I'd asked, trying to hold in creeping fear.

We were sitting at the corner of the racetrack, watching the running of a few fillies in training. His family were longtime race watchers, and they all seemed to have an innate interest and understanding of it.

He didn't answer right away. The fear grew, filled in around the edges of me.

For the last few years of our high school lives, Billy and I had talked about going to college together, maybe to the university here in town, or maybe one a little farther away so we could be with each other all the time, just us. We'd already sent our applications.

Never had we talked about *not* going to college.

But then Billy gave me a shy smile. Then he tucked a lank of wavy hair behind an ear, a nervous gesture I knew well. He did that onstage when he was anxious, afraid how a song would go.

The McGowan Brothers had recently teamed up with a manager, and that manager, Billy explained that day, was emphatic that the brothers make a name for themselves. Soon. That meant that they needed to move to New York.

I sat in a stupor, seeing our plan—me and Billy, four years together in college—was done. Over. I felt, at that minute, a sure death—the loss of a person who had known me like no one else had. Certainly not my parents.

"I want you to come with us," Billy said.

My whole world opened up when I heard that. My whole life. In a million tiny colored pieces I saw so many places we could go, people we could be, together.

It wasn't hard for me to decide that I would follow Billy and the McGowan Brothers to New York as soon as we graduated. Manhattan was the Holy Grail anyway, the place you shot for after you went to college. So why not just jump the gates and get there when you could? Especially when we had a lead, like we did with the McGowans' manager, especially when he was willing to help us find places to live, to fund everything.

Even my parents couldn't say no. My father had told me once on one of our long walks around town that he liked Billy very much and felt I should hang on to him—to our love. My father wanted, I saw then, for me to have what he and my mother had.

That was why my parents quickly assented to me following Billy. And that was why we were all brokenhearted when I messed it up.

A group of tourists came out of the pharmacy and started opening maps, apparently trying to decide where to go.

I pulled Baxter across the street and started walking, no destination in mind.

The phone rang again. I ignored it.

It rang again, and I pulled it out of my purse. *Gavin.* I tapped Reject.

I folded the magazine over so that only the article appeared.

After the marriage to Champlin fell apart, McGowan was linked for years to a young Mavis Regent.

That made me stop, grateful for a stoplight.

The McGowans' fame had skyrocketed right after they'd teamed with Mavis Regent. Mavis was a girl from Indiana who'd been named after Mavis Staples and who, similarly, could sing like a blues legend who'd been on the road for six decades. She was tiny and curvy, and she undulated her hips while she lolled her head side to side and belted out tunes that could scale from a thundering timber down to a smoky whisper. By the time the McGowans started touring with her, I had been Billy's girlfriend for nearly four years, and during that time I had become a master at watching live music, whether it was lounging in the studio, standing backstage or dancing out front. And so I couldn't help studying the guys around Mavis Regent. What I saw was that her bandmates, although they were much older than her, clearly loved working with her. The drummer, a wiry guy with a Mohawk, never took his eyes off her, all the while crashing and thumping, ready to change a beat at an instant's notice if she wanted. Her bass player, too, was often fixated on her. I wasn't surprised that Mick, Billy's brother, had a similar reaction, and definitely wasn't surprised when he and Mavis got together.

I was surprised, however, when *Billy* and Mavis did. In our new apartment.

The pain of finding them together had been unimaginable, and I was insane with anger. But I shouldn't ever have told Mick about it, because telling Mick was what brought about my downfall. Somehow in Mick's twisted mind I became the bad guy. Billy felt terrible—of course he did. He'd not only betrayed me but he'd betrayed his brother. Later, therapists would help me see that Billy's rejection of me, especially after I'd been arrested, was a way to make it up to Mick, to choose life with the band over me. And it was his ultimate rejection—not the arrest—that was the most painful memory.

"Oh, my God!" The sound broke my reverie.

I blinked. Four girls, likely high school–aged, rushed toward Baxy. "He's so cute! Oh, my God! Oh, my God!"

One of the girls stopped. She was shaking. "Is this Superdog?"

"It is," I said, glad for the diversion.

The girls squealed.

While they took pictures with Bax, I turned my back and kept reading the article.

Insiders say the end for McGowan and Champlin came when Champlin took possession of a large packet of cocaine, with intent to sell.

A shot of hot anger seared through me. The intent they mentioned *wasn't* true, but it didn't matter. Not now, not back then. Because when someone is caught with a certain amount of drugs, the law tacks on a conviction for intent to sell, not caring about your real motivation.

Still, I'd told my public defender a million times— I was there to *pick up* drugs. The person who usually did that for the McGowan Brothers was tending to some other emergency that day. At least that's what Mick, Billy's oldest brother, had told me when he asked me to do it.

I had agreed to *pick up* the drugs because I was falling—falling out of the McGowan world as their fame increased, falling out of Billy's world, too, despite how much we loved each other, how we'd essentially helped make each other.

I stood now on State Street, skimming the rest of the article. It made me sound like a drug abuser, or certainly an occasional drug user, neither of which was accurate. The piece ended with a promise to readers to keep investigating "whether Champlin is still in the drug world."

"Bye, Superdog!" The girls were all hugging him. They left and the light turned green. I tugged on Baxter's leash. But people recognized him now, and so we kept getting stopped. One person's noticing would trigger the next. "Superdog!" we'd hear and then someone, or many someones, would descend upon him with hugs and head-scratches, all of which Baxter loved.

I loved it, too, because such attention made Baxter happy. And mostly because it was a temporary distraction from the magazine (which I'd rolled tightly and tucked under my arm). Those moments with Baxter and people on the street allowed me to answer questions, normal everyday questions, about the breeder from whom I'd bought Baxter, the trainer I'd used in the city when he was a pup, the issue of crate versus bed, what kind of food he ate, how to order the collars and leashes, and so on.

No one seemed to have seen the article about me yet, likely no one really cared, but I was mortified, rattled.

The latest fans left. The weather was hotter than hell, but still I kept walking, unable to stop my feet. Instead of moving north to the park or east to the lake, which would provide respite from the heat, I decided to keep walking west. It felt almost like self-punishing instinct. We passed LaSalle, then Wells. I thought about walking around Old Town, but I associated that area with fun, with Sebastian.

Thank God Sebastian was on a story. For once, thank God that he was in a foreign country full of strife where the news of "Superdog's mom" wouldn't make a dent. I needed him to stay overseas while I attempted to come to terms with this.

I stopped in front of a parking garage, realizing I had to start merging my present and my past.

I had outrun the past for a long, long time. I usually felt as if that period of my life—falling in love with Billy and the downfall of us, of me—had happened to someone else. When I thought of it, I thought of *her*. I felt bad for *her*. I was embarrassed for *her*. I was glad not to think of *her* very often. And when I did it was as if I was telling myself a story about someone else, saw the tale scrolled out, almost like words in a book.

A horn blared. Baxter yipped. He was tugging on the leash, pulling me away from the entrance to the garage.

The phone rang. *Gavin.* I turned it off.

I let Baxter tug me down the street. He stopped a block later, wanting to smell something in a patch of grass. I let some slack go and watched Baxy sniff around, grateful that he would never understand any of this. Whereas before I had always wished Baxter could talk or communicate, now I was thankful he couldn't.

Her—she—was starting to be me again, and the merging of the two was exquisitely painful, and it was only made worse by my anticipation of the recognition in people's eyes when the story became widely circulated. I knew it wasn't big news. I knew it wasn't likely to change anyone's life. It would be fun news for some, others would say, *Who cares if she had a drug bust when she was eighteen? Who cares that she was married to a rock musician?*

The story wouldn't change anyone else's life. Except mine.

33

The morning after the article was released I met Gavin outside at Tempo Café. He was relentless with the phone calls. And it was either get a new phone or talk to him. (Although, getting a new phone was an option since I was starting to get calls from other media outlets. I'd changed the message, indicating people should contact Toni.) So I texted and said I would meet him. I wanted someplace public where I would be hesitant to lose my marbles in either a fit of screaming or a fit of tears. On the busy corner of State and Chestnut, the Tempo patio fit the bill. Most important, I could have Baxter near.

When we arrived, Baxter was strangely aloof with Gavin, maybe sensing my unease. When we sat Baxter didn't seek out his usual spot under the table. Instead, he tucked himself under my chair, almost behind me.

"I cannot take not knowing you," Gavin blurted, as if he'd been holding in the words.

I finally allowed myself to focus on those brown eyes, but the sight of them made me wince. Not only were they full of pain, but the love that I'd started to feel when I saw those eyes was still there. It felt like a punch to the gut.

"You are the best thing that's ever happened to me," he said. He kept talking, and I couldn't look at his eyes. I only watched his mouth move.

"I can't believe you!" I finally said, interrupting his rambling, my words biting and hard, so laden with emotion they surprised me. "All the time we spent together… That was…fake? Were you just trying to get a story?" Had my instincts turned so bad?

"Of course not."

I remembered the time we met. "Were you looking for me that day we met at the park? Were you targeting me?"

"What? No!"

"Right, of course not," I said sarcastically.

"I saw you in the park. I thought you were hot. And then I came a little closer, watching you and Baxy."

I wanted to smack him for using Baxter's nickname.

"And then I *knew* you were hot," he continued. "And then those guys came up to us and *then* I realized who you were."

"And then you exploited me. Because you wanted

to be a writer. Like Sebastian." Somehow I knew this would hurt Gavin, and I was right.

He gritted his teeth. "Yes, at first I was fishing for a story that would get me working on the other side of the magazine. Yes." He breathed out hard. "But I fell for you."

"Sure you did." I choked back a sudden sob. I shook my head. "All that we did together, the sex we had, all the time you spent with Baxter…" I put my hand over my eyes. I had a whole new shame now. "That was all for the story. It was all bullshit."

Some child's voice inside my head said, *I knew it. I knew it. I knew this would happen.*

"Not true," he said. "I love Baxter. And I think I love you."

I half laughed and half choked. "You 'think.' That's priceless." I rewound to the day in the park. "Did you really have a dog named Wrigley that died?"

"Yes," he answered fast, a little irritated. "I did not make up Wrigley."

"So then what did you make up?"

Silence.

"That first night we spent together," I said, remembering. "The next day you made me French toast. How did you know my dad used to make French toast?"

"I didn't! You told me."

I scoffed, although he was right.

"I don't know how to explain this," he said, sighing. "But yes, after that first night at my place, after you left, I fished around, just curious for information about you, and I was curious about Sebastian, too. But it seemed like nothing was there, not in terms of any good stories."

"And so?"

"And then we started dating and I dropped it. Then, out of curiosity because I was into you, I fished around some more. And then I found the story of your marriage to Billy McGowan and your arrest. I didn't do anything at first, but after the accident, after seeing you and Sebastian, I gave them to the editor. But by that point I really had fallen for you."

"Uh-huh. Well, that's a funny way to show it."

He winced.

"And you didn't ask me about it? You just gave the story to your editor? Even though you had 'fallen' for me?"

"I told the editor, then I regretted it." Another sigh. "I told her drop to it. But she wouldn't. Too hot a story."

"I'm not talking about the editor—*your* editor now—I'm talking about decisions you made. *You.*"

I looked around the restaurant, populated with either couples or groups of people, many of whom had clearly been out the night before and were still living through the fun of it—laughing over omelets the size of basketballs. God, I so wished I was them.

"Did you try to stop it? Did you even *try?*" I heard the incredulousness in my own voice.

He shook his head. "I didn't," he said. "I really couldn't. And even if I could…"

"Even if you could, what?"

"I was too afraid to lose my job."

I felt almost as if he had shot me. Baxter even flinched, cowered for a second and then looked around, suspicious, as if he, too, had felt a jolt.

He seemed so weak to me then. He looked, to my eyes, pale, and even his chocolate-brown eyes had dimmed, gone gray. I could feel Sebastian then, in part because I viewed him as a strong man, one with integrity. Unlike the one before me. But also, I couldn't ignore that I was losing another man to his profession.

I reached under the table and stroked Baxter's head. This was the end of something for him, too— of having another dad. That thought tore through me, as well. Poor Baxy.

"Well, I'm glad you didn't lose your job," I said to Gavin, standing. "The job you hated so much. But you've lost me."

34

I thought I was Baxter's bodyguard, but after the article came out, I noticed it was the other way around. Or at least I noticed that the bodyguard business works both ways.

By 4:00 p.m. two days after Gavin told me about the article, I had forty-seven unanswered phone calls, seventy unchecked messages and fifty-two texts I hadn't looked at. And that was even with the message directing people to Toni. And they were growing. It was time to shake off the doldrums.

I called the temp service that I'd been using for assistants and hired one, agreeing to pay the agency what seemed an exorbitant fee to respond to all calls and emails. I called the graphic design people for my website and updated them on the situation.

Then I started tackling the messages. A number of them were from Toni herself. I pulled up everything from her and read them all.

They started with energized texts—No publicity

is bad publicity! Let's use this and go from here!— and progressed to messages of concern.—You okay? Call me?

I didn't call Toni back yet. I couldn't decide how to handle this. As if seeing my blank stare, Baxter ran toward the door and barked. *Let's go out!* He'd been doing this for the past day, even though I'd taken him out a few times since our last meal with Gavin the day before. It was as if he were testing me, and if I didn't respond, he would find a ball and toss it at my feet. He'd pant, looking from the ball to me and back again. *You all right? You all right?*

When we went outside, we stuck to the alleys in the Gold Coast. They tended to be surprisingly (relatively) clean (unless you were behind one of the bars on Division Street). Trash and recycling bins had, for the most part, been emptied, and there was only minimal detritus along the back of condo buildings and homes.

Of course, we still passed people sometimes. Like the good security detail he was, Baxter wouldn't respond right away. If someone stopped and yelled "Superdog!" he sometimes let himself be scratched on the head for a minute, but always he was looking at me. He seemed to be saying, *Is this okay?* And again, I thought I could hear him ask, *You all right?*

Meanwhile, I felt relieved that it was Superdog they were interested in, not Superdog's mom and her troubling past.

And then Baxter would cut it short. He would not go into his social mode, dropping the ball at someone's feet, letting them scratch his back now or kiss his black nose. Often he would duck down a side alley or a street if he saw people coming.

It was as if he picked up something strange about me, about *us*. And whenever I got up in the middle of the night, which was often, Bax was there for me. I could see him in the streetlight that seeped through my drapes. He'd look at me with a heavy-lidded expression that said, *What? What is it?*

"It's nothing, Baxy," I'd say, rubbing one of his ears, the way he liked.

But still he'd look at me, concerned.

"Go back to sleep," I'd say.

If I didn't fall back asleep, I'd get up to try and shake the mental noise, rather than wrestle with it alone in the dark. Sometimes I headed for the kitchen. I made tea and looked out the window. Other times I went to my office, sat on the couch and read a book, something light, hoping it lifted my mood and sent me back to bed. But wherever my mind was in the midnight ramblings or afternoon walks or the one brief visit to the studio, Bax insisted he be there—sitting at my feet when I was drinking tea, lying with his head on my lap when I read, and often, maybe always, he'd look up and study my face.

Every time, I'd say again, *It's nothing, Bax.*

Such a lie.

35

On the fifth day, I picked up Toni's call. "We have to get a statement out there or we lose it," she said.

I paused, waiting. But she didn't chastise me for not returning her texts and messages.

"We lose what?" I said.

"The publicity."

"Good," I said, "let's lose it."

"The thing is if we don't speak now…"

I loved how Toni spoke as if we'd been having the same conversation for days. She hadn't yet asked any questions about the arrest, or my marriage to Billy. She hadn't asked if I was okay which I deeply, deeply appreciated.

"…if we don't speak now, the story is out there, and it's the last bit of information out there for you, and that means it's the only thing out there for you. We need something else."

I didn't say anything.

"Hey," Toni said, and even though she'd spoken

only one word I could hear her voice was low, kind. "You have to think of I'd Rather Sleep with the Dog. We've put too much into this."

It was the "we" that made me stand.

I stood for a second more, then as Toni continued to talk about how much she loved the business and how much she wanted it to succeed, I felt a charge. I crossed my living room, picking up the studio keys from the side table where I'd left them days ago. *What I need is to get to work, not simply hire people to push it around. What I need is to be alive again. I need to get back to what I love.*

And I realized in that instant that I *did* truly love what I was doing with Baxter—I loved designing dogwear, I loved working with my dog. These were the things that had been mainly responsible for me feeling alive. That alive feeling wasn't all Gavin.

"You're right," I said to Toni. "Let's get on it, issue a statement, whatever you want to do."

"Yeah?"

"Yeah."

"That a girl! Meet me at my favorite new place—" she named a cross street "—and we'll hammer it out."

Toni's favorite new place was, conveniently, a block from my house, something I was sure Toni had orchestrated so as not to overwhelm me. But it was a true find—a hole-in-the-wall piano bar. Because they didn't serve food, she told me, I could bring the dog.

When we got there, Toni hugged me, kissed Baxter, then launched into explanations about branding and about "owning your shit."

We sat, she waved away a waiter, then typed on her laptop, fingers clacking. "Let's just get to the point with the press release," she said.

"Please," I said.

"What about something like this? 'I have made some mistakes in my personal life, and for those I am sorry.'" She looked up at me.

I nodded. "Should we add something about whether I did drugs?"

Toni blinked a few times. "Well…what would you say?"

"I'd say, 'I have never taken drugs in my life, nor do I condone the usage of them.'"

"I love it." More clacking of her fingers. "Although let's take out the condoning part. Sounds a little judgy."

"Great."

Toni wrote more, read it to me, I'd comment and then we'd revise. Sentence by sentence we worked.

"Almost done," Toni said.

Something about being with Toni and her efficient strength gave me some strength.

My phone lit up. I looked at the display—it was the front desk of my condo building.

I scrolled through my phone and saw that they had called three times since Bax and I had left the building. Occasionally, the doormen called just to say a package had arrived, especially once they knew I was working on the dogwear and often waiting for materials to arrive. But most of the supplies went to the studio or the plant now.

"Hello?"

"There's a William here for you," the doorman said, skipping his usual introduction.

"William?" I repeated. "I don't know a William."

"He says his name is William," the doorman said, voice lower. "But he's…you know…?"

"I don't know."

"He's…"

I think my mind caught up with the doorman almost at the same time. But he beat me to the words.

"Bill," the doorman said. Then he murmured, "Billy."

I opened my mouth and closed it. Then, like I'd seen Baxter do so many times, I cocked my head to the side.

"Billy McGowan," the doorman said, a now emphatic whisper. "I think he's trying to fly under the radar, but I figured it out."

I looked at Baxter.

I looked at Toni.

"Billy McGowan is in my lobby," I said to fill her in, to confirm.

Her eyes widened.

"Yes!" the doorman said.

"Well, what does he want?"

"He simply asked for you."

"He simply asked for me," I repeated. I would have loved to hear those words from Billy if they'd been delivered at a different time in my life.

But it was too late.

"Tell him I'm not home and can't see him," I said.

Toni shook her head no and grasped her hands around her neck as if choking herself. I closed my eyes so I couldn't see her.

A pause, then the doorman said, "Ma'am?"

I repeated myself.

I heard the doorman speaking away from the phone. Then a muffled question and reply.

"Sir!" I heard the doorman say, and then muffled sounds as the phone shifted hands.

Then…

Then…

His voice when he came on the phone was the same. "Please, Jess," he said. "Please."

36

When I got back to my building I changed my mind ten times about whether I wanted to see Billy. I came in the garage exit, then just stood there, letting Baxy sniff around someone's bike. I was there for at least fifteen minutes trying to think, then trying to silence my thoughts, but my mind just ran like a hamster wheel.

I finally entered the building, bypassing the lobby, and went upstairs. I let Baxter inside the condo, rushed around trying to spruce up my lank hair, threw on a shortish skirt and wedge heels. I changed my mind again and again about whether to go downstairs. The doorman had texted me twice and called once to say that Billy was in the lobby. The same doorman hadn't let friends wait for me in the lobby when I was five minutes away from the place, but Billy's star power had apparently done the trick.

Finally it seemed silly to ignore him—he was, after all, the reason for the hundreds of messages and emails we'd gotten, the trending, again, of the Superdog video because of Superdog's mom's troubles.

The elevator ride down was an interminable process. I entered the lobby, but I stopped short. I inhaled deeply and then I saw him on the other side of the room. I only needed that brief second to take in the dirty-blond hair, shorter now than it used to be, to recognize Billy. I stepped behind a tall plant.

Why is he here? In this city? At my place?

I had never imagined a situation where I would see him again, no matter how small the world got, or how big. No matter how many friends we had in common on some social network, there was no way our worlds would coincide again. I had to believe that was true in order to believe I could live without him. When he'd begun to slip away, it had been terrifying. After I got arrested and Billy announced we were done, I had to get my head around the fact that no one would understand me like he had. My shot for having what my parents had was gone. He was gone.

I squeezed my eyes shut. I made myself open them, allowing shock to register again at the image of Billy. Billy McGowan. I expected him to be, decades after I'd known him, well…puffy. But although he was broader across the chest than he used to be, he looked to be in great shape. I closed my eyes again.

And right when I did so, *bam!* I was hit, simultaneously, with so many memories of him and me. Life quickly flipped through a stack of snapshots—

each lighting my brain for an instant, then flashing away, another bursting into its place.

I saw me and Billy in his parents' basement, could actually feel how his hands felt on my hips, that first time he drew me to him. He was so slim then, our hip bones touched.

I saw us walking through the halls of our high school, hands clasped.

I saw us in his first car, one of the few items in his life that wasn't a hand-me-down, hadn't been filtered through his brothers or family. I saw us in that car, hands clasped between the seats, remembering the thrill of his flesh, rougher than mine.

I saw the backstage, after one of the first real gigs I attended—Billy coming through the stage door, his face lit with wonder, happiness. And when he saw me, the marvel and joy on his face somehow increased. I knew it, and I saw it and I didn't doubt it.

I saw us at a dinner with his family, exchanging frequent smiles, giddy in the knowledge that we had each other.

I saw Billy and me at a school dance shortly after we'd decided not to go to college. We drifted around the hardwood floor, draped on each other.

For some reason, that memory made me realize I was still in the lobby, standing on its hardwood floor, hiding behind a plant. I knew if I hadn't yet been spotted by Billy or the doorman, it would only be a matter of moments before I was.

When I opened my eyes again, I felt a little dizzy.

Yes, that was Billy McGowan.

He looked up from his phone and around the lobby.

His head swiveled to the right as if to look toward the door, but then it froze. His face swung toward me and he stopped. I saw his eyes then, as if I were right in front of him.

His mouth parted, and I knew he saw me, even if I was mostly hidden by the plant.

I stepped to the right. Then I stepped farther to the right until I was in full view. The doorman wasn't at the desk for some reason. No one else was in the lobby.

I felt exposed, almost violently so, as though I had stepped naked into a freezing-cold valley. The feeling almost made me flinch, want to fall to the ground.

Somewhere along the line Billy must have decided to remain, in part, an innocent. He had always been that, being the youngest, but a lot of people who had that quality lost it. Yet he smiled now, and I saw a childlike curiosity still present. Our eyes met.

"Jessica," he said.

He stood. He took a step, then another and another and another.

37

Later, I would think of that hour Billy and I spent in my lobby as idyllic, despite the fact that at the time I thought the worst had happened. My past had shown up on my figurative doorstep.

We talked softly at first, really nothing more than "Hello." And "How are you?"

A maintenance man replaced the doorman for a break, and I saw him recognize Billy. Saw him recognize me. But he was trained well by the building management. He immediately launched into an apparent plethora of tasks, studiously avoiding us with his eyes or taking himself out of the lobby again.

And so Billy and I kept talking.

"I couldn't believe it when I saw it," Billy said eventually, speaking about the Superdog video. "Or I guess I should say I couldn't believe it when I heard it. When I heard your voice."

"What do you mean? Why?" I didn't know how to do much but ask questions.

"I was with my kid that weekend."

"Your kid? Oh, that's right." My eyes went on an autoblink function, but some part of me understood the information. I'd read a few years ago that Billy had gotten his makeup artist/girlfriend pregnant, and they had been together a few years before breaking up.

Billy nodded. "We call him Will."

"Will," I said. "I like that. Will McGowan."

Billy's eyes were never as clear as they were at that moment, his smile never so wide. "I am in love with the kid."

"I'm glad."

He said something about Will and the "minimally sane" relationship with Will's mom.

"So I was with Will for the weekend," he said, "and I was in the studio, and I was letting him play with a tablet. He was watching videos. I never really hear them anymore but then…" He paused, looked at me. "Then I heard your voice."

I sat there and looked at him. "So you saw the video of Baxter *before* the magazine article about us came out?" I wasn't sure why I was so keen to know, but this seemed important.

Billy nodded. "Will kept playing it. He kept shrieking and laughing. Then he'd yell, 'Baxter! Baxter!' along with you. *You.* I think I knew it was you before I asked him for the video to see for myself. And then there you were on the screen, running across the street, as beautiful as ever, apologizing to that mom, sweet as ever."

I sat back on the lobby couch. A woman I knew from the same floor came in the front doors and waved. She glanced at Billy. And stopped. Just stopped dead in her tracks.

The neighbor pointed and mouthed, *Billy McGowan?*

There was no point in denying it. I nodded. She made a big-eyed, excited expression, gave me the thumbs-up, then moved toward the elevators.

"That's funny you've seen the Superdog video," I said, not knowing where to go from there.

"About ten million times. But I'm not the only one, Jess. *Everyone* has seen that video."

"Yeah, seems like it, doesn't it?"

"Jess, seriously," Billy said, "people in other countries have seen Baxter's video. I did a couple of concerts overseas and I saw it in Asia. I saw it in the Middle East!"

"C'mon."

"I'm not kidding!"

I nodded. I couldn't figure out what to say, or even why to say it. I didn't know what to make of his presence or his words.

He seemed to sense my confusion. He told me about his family, not mentioning Mick, then asked me about my parents. We kept catching each other up on our lives.

"It was good, wasn't it?" Billy said.

"'It' meaning what?"

"Us."

Us. I felt a crazy zing rip through me, a fourteen-year-old girl's thrill at that word.

"It was good when it was good."

"When it was good," Billy repeated.

I'd started getting suspicious with Billy about five months after we got married, four months after we'd gone on tour. I knew him too well. I knew he was hiding something. It was the way he spoke with certain girls after shows, clearly not just people he knew through meet and greets but rather people who knew each other.

I watched him once while he spoke to a girl at a gig. She was adorable. She looked like someone I would want to be friends with. *Has she been at our place? In our bed?*

My suspicions led me to arranging our medicine cabinet like a curator. I figured if he was cheating, bringing home the occasional groupie, at least the items in the medicine cabinet would say, *Someone lives here, someone permanent.* I tried to put in the forefront of the cabinet things that indicated a woman lived in that apartment, a woman who only needed minor products to enhance herself but who was also fashionable and cool. It became a weird obsession—as if it would make any difference. I started shopping for items that other women would see. Two lipsticks were usually main-

stays, both in enameled tubes with carved floral designs on the top. They sat near a silver-plated hairbrush
that had its own case. I found a tiny marigold-colored
compact at a vintage store in Greenwich Village, its
cover etched with silver lines.

Later it was more obvious that he was cheating. I
found things like the condom wrappers and the er-
rant earring under the bed.

And then I found Mavis there.

"Did you want me to find you and her?" I said
now. In Chicago. In my lobby.

He didn't have to ask who I was speaking of.

"No!" he said. He kept shaking his head. "I didn't
want you to know. I hated myself for it."

And so, after all those years, we finally talked
about his infidelities.

Billy apologized. "I would be *nothing* without
your encouragement," he said. When I remained silent, still, he said, "I needed you for my creativity."
Still I said nothing. "For my life," he finished.

I let it sit. I had to. I had gotten so good at being
alive, staying in the moment. And now I couldn't
help but process everything, process that I was with
my ex-husband, fifteen years after our breakup, long
after our dirty laundry (*my* dirty laundry) had been
aired. We had been outed.

"I sometimes wonder if maybe I wanted out of that
life," I said. "But I didn't have the strength to do it.

Maybe I wanted to be caught—forced to be myself again, to re-create myself."

I took a breath. I filled my lungs. I checked in on my heart and got a wallop of pain when I thought about Gavin. Then everything veered again into today.

"So what happened with you?" I asked. I let the question be unspecific. I wasn't sure what I really wanted to ask him.

Billy was looking at me, seeming to search my eyes. Then, as if he couldn't take what he saw there, he reached out. I held my breath. He put his face in his right hand. How many times had I seen that gesture? I knew it wasn't studied. I knew it meant Billy was struggling. And why did that make me feel good?

"I'm sorry," he said. His voice sounded strangled. "I'm sorry it happened. I'm sorry I got defensive about Mick."

"He's your brother," I said. "Your bandmate."

"He was. They were," Billy said. "But you were my heart."

That hurt so bad I almost moaned out loud.

"You heard the band broke up?" he asked.

I nodded. Even after all that had happened, the news of the band's split when I'd read it had saddened me. Because even if I was no longer a part of them, wasn't allowed to be, I'd hoped their bonds and their music would fuel them, sustain them.

"Are you still close?"

"Kevin and me," he said. "Not Mick."

"I'm sorry."

A small shrug, one too understated for the fact that Billy no longer spoke to his oldest brother, the one who had gotten him into music, the person Billy had always wanted to be.

"Are you heartbroken?" I asked.

It was a bold question. We both felt it. We both knew that my demise had been orchestrated, in a way, by Mick.

"I was," Billy said. "I'm moving past it."

My phone dinged a few times. I looked down. People often talk about how bad news is delivered— *the call came out of nowhere; it was such a normal day.*

My day was not normal. There was nothing normal about seeing your old lover, your ex-husband, for the first time since a long horrible time ago. And yet I saw some kind of simplicity in that scene—Billy and I speaking in low tones in my lobby.

My phone rang. Then rang again. The screen read, *Barbara.* Sebastian's mother.

I answered, mostly in an effort to show Billy what a wildly functioning person I was—I could be in the midst of a shocker of a conversation like this and still take a call.

"Hey, Barb," I said in a cheery tone

"Jess," she said. She never called me that. She

wasn't one for nicknames. Sebastian's brother was always Thomas, never Tom.

I was about to ask how she was, but then she spoke again.

"Sebastian has been arrested. Detained, they say."

"They?"

"The Libyan government."

38

My world imploded, corroded, then exploded again.

"Detained?" I said incredulously. "Arrested?"

Sebastian's mom wailed, the cry piercing me, waking me up.

"I'll call you right back," I said.

I stood. Billy did the same, blinking, confused.

"Thanks for coming, Billy," I said. "But I have to go."

"Why?" He smiled, and I remembered that smile, the one that said, *I can talk you into this. I know how to get through to you.*

"My husband has been arrested overseas," I said.

"I thought you were divorced."

"I am." Something hit me then, a realization—I had insisted on breaking up with Sebastian in part because of the fear that something like this would happen. Now that it had. Strangely. Strangely…

I sat down on the lobby chair.

I took a breath and took stock of myself. I had always feared these potentials about Sebastian—that he would be kidnapped, killed, tortured. And yet I was, I realized then, slightly fine right now; I was even grateful Barb had called me. I was glad to be kept abreast of it, if "it" was going to happen.

I focused on Billy's questioning face.

"I have the dog upstairs." I waved vaguely at the ceiling. Somehow I'd forgotten about Baxter when I was talking with Billy. He'd always been able to make me see only him.

I left Billy and ran up ten flights of stairs. I'd taken the stairs only once before when there had been a fire in an upstairs apartment and we'd been evacuated. I couldn't have taken the elevator now if I wanted to because…because…I felt the need. To run to something? From something? I didn't know.

Baxter was just inside my door, fairly bouncing, as if he, too, sensed an emergency.

He barked, jumped, barked again.

"Baxter, stop!" My voice was loud, shrill. Baxy shrunk away from me, cowering.

"I'm sorry, good dog," I said, crouching to pick him up.

I kissed his neck. I whispered, "Sebastian…" then let my voice die away.

But he whined, whimpered, as if to say, *Tell me*.

"Something's happened."

Holding him, I went into the kitchen and called

Sebastian's mom. "Hi. It's me again. What happened?"

"I got a call from the paper," she said, sounding more reined in now, although how could she be? "He and his cameraman picked up a translator and a driver, and they were going to interview rebels, but they were stopped by a roadblock and taken by the police."

"Okay," I said, like, *Okay, I can handle this.* Could I? Here was what I'd always wondered. "Do we know why they were picked up? What they're alleging?"

"No."

We were quiet a second.

"Thanks for calling me." Technically, I wasn't Sebastian's wife anymore. I wasn't his emergency contact. I wasn't, legally, anything at all to him.

"Of course." Barbara made a little whimper. "I have to stop crying." She took a breath and exhaled loudly. "But we can't talk about this to anyone else. That's what they say."

"Do they know you were going to tell me?" I wasn't sure why I asked that. *Who were "they," exactly?*

"Yes. They said I shouldn't tell anyone. But I knew you would want to know, and I knew Sebastian would want you to know."

"Thank you," I said. We both paused again. "How do you know that?"

I thought of conversations Sebastian and I had

had, about his job and its dangers, especially when I couldn't know anything about his assignments.

"I think you're one of the best people to handle a crisis," Sebastian had said. "I watch you handle them all day."

"But those are *styling* choices," I'd said, knowing I was shortchanging myself even as I said it. "Those decisions are only about whether to lose the scarf or keep the scarf *and* the earrings."

"Don't belittle what you do," he'd said.

The oft-occurring conversational tango, when we discussed his job, and I negatively compared mine to his, was one of the last steps of the dance Sebastian and I would make. Then we would round to his job again, to the demands it posed that I saw as too great.

"I have a great job," he would say. "Even you think that."

"It *is* a great job," I would say.

"But you don't want me to do it."

I didn't often respond to that. How would you tell someone (who you love so very much) not to do the thing that they love?

"I wish you weren't such a thrill seeker," I'd say.

"So what if I am?" Sebastian would say. We had debated the point, discussed the point, philosophized about the point. And yet he always humored me, kept discussing it.

Sebastian was usually the first to make a suggestion. Could I accept and support his position, that his job was necessary to tell the stories no one else was going to hear, to tell about the people in various regions, caught unawares, *their* lives hemorrhaging with risk?

"Every day they're on the edge of dying," he'd said. His face strained. "*Every* day. And meanwhile, when I'm there I'm staying in the freaking Kabul Serena Hotel, where I can get a massage every day if I want it." He had shaken his head, the strain intensifying.

And now…now that Sebastian had been detained by a foreign government…now that he was at the same edge as those people he spoke about, I could look back on that argument and with crystalline recognition see that his expression had been not only strained it had also been one of despair. It hurt him for me to not understand why he needed to be there, to tell these stories, how hard it was to stay at the "freaking Kabul Serena" when people were dying outside. How had I been so shortsighted and unable to see it?

My memories were drawn away by the sound of Barbara, over the phone line, sighing loudly, sounding as if she was trying to keep it together.

"How are you?" I asked.

She ignored the question. "He really loves you, Jess," she said.

I went still, quiet. Not just in my words but in my

whole body and mind. Like an animal. "Thanks for saying that."

"I'm not just saying it." Barbara had been jealous-seeming at times, especially when Sebastian and I had been exuberantly happy.

"He always said how hard it was to keep secrets from you," Barbara said. "He knew you didn't like it, and he didn't, either."

"It's part of the job," I said, repeating the sentence Sebastian often had.

"Yes." She breathed out. "He's said that since he first started writing for the paper in New York. It's part of the job."

I took a breath. "Barbara, has the newspaper notified the government?"

I remembered our first year in Chicago when Sebastian was making an effort to share things with me, and he'd shown me disclaimer paperwork that he had to sign with the paper, assuming his own risks, agreeing that his "heirs and assigns" would not have the right to sue "in the case of death or injury." It also indicated that in a situation of detainment overseas, the newspaper would make every effort to work in tandem with the U.S. government, whatever agencies were involved.

"Yes," Barbara said. "They say they're working together. They think they know what region he's in."

I tried to imagine Sebastian. Was he in a steel cell or was it a room with dirt floors, the kind he'd seen in Pakistan and told me about? *After* he'd traveled, *after* he'd researched the story, *after* it had been published, he would tell me about what he'd seen. Now I realized I might have understood more than I'd given myself credit for.

"They have pictures of them," his mom continued. "Their faces, with a newspaper from yesterday to show the date."

"How do they look?"

"I didn't want to see them."

"I do," I said, surprising myself. I paused, checked in. "I want to see the pictures." This time I sounded sure.

39

Outside the window of Billy's town car, Lake Michigan blurred by. *Look at those people,* I thought. *They're just sitting on the beach.* I found the concept endearing, the pockets of people on the sand. They seemed miles away.

When I'd gotten back to the lobby, Billy was still there. He was speaking to the doorman, who looked simultaneously thrilled to be talking to Billy McGowan and also stressed about not screwing up his job.

"Jess," Billy said.

"This is Baxter."

Billy smiled and shook Baxter's paw, the one that hung over my arm as I held him. I couldn't seem to put him down, his doggy-weight too soothing to give up.

I looked at the doorman. "Could you call me a cab?" Hailing cabs on the street with a dog was difficult, even with Superdog.

"Let me take you where you're going," Billy said. "I have a car outside."

"No, it's fine," I said.

Yes, sure, all is fine. I nodded at the doorman who picked up the phone.

"Jess, let me," Billy said.

I shook my head, but looked at him as he continued to talk.

"I didn't help you," he said. His eyes seemed to get misty for a moment. "I didn't help you. And I still hate myself for that."

"Billy," I said, my voice worried. "You don't have to do this. Please."

"Minimum fifteen minutes until taxi arrival, ma'am," the doorman said. Technically, it wasn't such a long time, but I needed to get to Barb's house. I needed to know what was happening with Sebastian.

"You'll give me a ride?" I said to Billy.

"Of course."

Five minutes later, we were speeding north on Lake Shore Drive. For a while we were quiet. But I wanted to talk about something. Anything, really. Just for a break from the anxiety about Sebastian.

"What are you in town for?" I said to Billy.

He was staring through the window. Didn't look at me. But he said, "You. To make sure you're okay."

"That's nice," I said. "But other than me…"

"That's it."

"You're not in town playing or promoting something?"

"Just you, Jess." His words were kind. "I saw the stupid article in that magazine, and everything came back. I had to find you. To see if I could help or make things better."

Oddly, I felt his friendship then. I had missed that.

"Do you have people with you?" I asked.

By the end of my time with Billy, the McGowan Brothers never traveled without staff. And given the continued success of the band and now Billy's solo career, it seemed likely.

"Just my assistant," he said. "She has family here, so…"

The car's GPS spoke, and Billy's driver headed west.

The neighborhood had been rough-and-tumble when Barb and her husband had raised a family there, but it was largely gentrified now. Brick buildings that used to house three flats were now single-family. Manicured bushes and flowers abounded.

Years ago, Sebastian had taken me to the house he'd grown up in, a bungalow a few blocks away. He'd pointed at it from the car, had said fondly that it was *covered in linoleum*.

When we neared Barb's current house I told the driver how to maneuver the one-way streets around the place, then I looked at Billy.

"Thank you," I said.

"Thank *you*," he said. I recognized the sincerity there, the Billy I used to know.

And I wondered if he saw me. I thought I'd changed after my arrest, but maybe some of our core always remained. Maybe someday I would get to ask Billy about my core, the me deep down—whether he still saw it, whether I had ever had it. But I had more immediate issues.

"There it is at the end of the block," I said to the driver, pointing at Barb's house.

"We'll wait for you," Billy said.

"No. I really don't want you to do that."

"Why?"

"Because this has to do with Sebastian and me. And his family. I don't want to bring my stuff into it." I waved a hand between Billy and me.

And strangely, rather than feeling the starting twinge of disgrace—the way I usually felt when I thought about Billy, about my arrest, about Billy and me—I felt okay.

"Then I'll go to the hotel," Billy said, "and I'll have the driver come back to wait for you. Down the street," he added before I could say something. "Really. I don't need the car the rest of the day."

"Okay," I said.

I took the help.

Although Barbara hadn't moved too far from the old neighborhood, she'd moved up. When Sebastian's dad had died of a long battle with cancer, his life insurance policy allowed Barbara to quit working and buy herself a new house. As a result, she was now in a gray-stone home with a tinkling waterfall and manicured lawn in front.

It was six in the evening by the time Billy dropped us off, and the city had cooled considerably. Barbara sat on the front stoop, something I couldn't recall seeing her do before. She was a fit woman who played tennis four times a week, her brown hair curled under at her shoulders. Her face was woven with delicate lines, but it was easy to see how pretty she'd been and still was.

"Baxter!" Barbara said when we were out of the car. Billy swiftly closed the door and the car pulled away, just like I'd asked.

Baxter bounded up to Barb and into her arms, licking her face, making her laugh.

I walked up a few steps and sat down beside them.

"Ah, that felt good," Barbara said, settling Baxter down on her lap. "I haven't been kissed like that in a long time, longer than I want to admit. And I know I haven't laughed since…" Her voice died away. She closed her mouth.

"Since?" I said.

"It must have been recently," Barbara said. "I mean, I laugh. I do. But…"

I put a hand over one of hers, which rested on her knee. "But it's hard to imagine when."

"Yes. This takes over everything."

We fell silent. Baxter got up and began to sniff around Barbara's hedges.

"They say it's going to rain," Barbara said.

I said nothing.

"They're emailing me the photo," Barbara said. "I told them you wanted to see."

"Thank you."

"I still can't."

"I understand." I paused. "Do we know where Sebastian is? Like what city or village?" I asked.

"Just Libya," she said.

I imagined it on a map. "It's a big country."

"I know." Barbara waved a hand at her house. "The laptop is on the kitchen counter, and it's opened to my email."

40

I was only two steps into Barb's house when I halted, froze. Then I inched across the hardwood floors, pulled by a frame of black, light glinting off a small pane of glass. That glass covered a photo of Sebastian and his mom. It was taken on a sailboat in Lake Michigan—they both looked ecstatically happy. Likely it had been taken by his dad.

I took another step. Sebastian not only appeared happy in the image, he looked young. He looked completely unweighed—no responsibilities, no stories pressing on his unconscious.

I tossed my hair over my shoulder, put a hand to my brow that felt hot. I had other more important photos to view.

I turned and stared at Barbara's laptop, sitting on the kitchen's granite bar. I walked to it and took a seat at the high stool. I felt too high up, suddenly, and I wanted to be grounded. I thought of taking the laptop to the table, but it occurred to me that all this had likely just begun. Likely, I was going to continue to encounter situations where my equilibrium felt off. I might as well practice keeping calm while doing it.

I breathed in and out a few times, and then I was ready as I could be.

The computer was open to Barbara's in-box, which looked mostly full of emails from family. I looked toward the top. There it was—second one.

I clicked open the email, scanning it.

…the situation in Syria, in which your son Sebastian Hess and his photographer, Bill Baxter, were detained by local government. Please be assured that we are taking every step to resolve this. We are here to answer any questions you may have.

Attached is the photo we received from the captors. It has not yet been authenticated, but we will let you know when that occurs. In the interim, please let us know if you would like to discuss. Our sympathies are with you and your family, although we hope for a positive result in this trying situation.

Very truly yours,

Beverly Holkins

My first thought was that Beverly Holkins sounded like a lovely woman, and I was glad the government hired seemingly kind people, especially when that woman had some responsibility in finding Sebastian Hess. Or at least keeping us apprised of the search for him.

Then I kept looking at the other name mentioned in the email. *Bill Baxter.* The photographer Sebastian had worked with, one he had so much respect for that he wanted to name our dog after him. I hadn't realized they still teamed up. I clicked on the attachment, grateful when it seemed to need an extra few seconds to download. Then it opened across the screen.

Sebastian. And the other man I'd never seen. But now I remembered Sebastian's description of him. *He's got blond hair,* Sebastian had said. *In fact, it's nearly the color of Baxter's.* But Bill Baxter's hair was graying at the temples. Bill Baxter looked very scared.

I decided not to make guesses about anything. I drew my eyes immediately to the left, to Sebastian. He was crouched, his back against a lumpen brown wall. He wore the Converse sneakers he always had on when he left for an assignment. Ditto the dark gray jacket with a bunch of zippers (it held lots of stuff and could be repurposed to be a few different garments). I peered at his eyes. I thought I'd be able to read everything there, every thought or fear or plan. But they just looked like dark dots, rather than the mesmerizing hazel I loved.

Bill Baxter was crouching, too. His face bore a somewhat stern but mostly tired expression. He wore an army-green vest with pockets that looked recently depleted, almost puffed with air.

I heard Barbara come inside. "Don't worry," she

called to me. "I'm not coming in there. I'm going to lie down and try to take a nap. I've got the phone."

"Good, Barbara," I called.

"You should lie down, too. This could be a long day."

"It's not already?"

"Ha," she said.

"Ha," I said.

Neither of us acknowledged what was perfectly clear   that this "day" could be many, or weeks or months.

"I've got Baxter," she said. "Is that okay?"

"Of course. He's a good snuggler."

"That's exactly what I need."

I marveled that we could have this conversation. That we could inject even a little bit of levity or normalcy into the moment.

"You really should rest when you get a chance," she said, her voice sailing through the otherwise silent home. I wondered if it was quiet where Sebastian was. Or if the air there was filled with sounds, screams, screeching, fear.

"Not just yet." I turned back to the laptop.

I drew my attention to Sebastian again. The person who had taken the photo must have been about ten feet from the men leaning against the wall, so the detail of the picture was a bit fuzzy. *Why,* I wondered then, *had they made them crouch? Why not let them stand? Shouldn't there be mug shots if they'd been arrested?*

I studied the top of Sebastian's head, then his fore-head, then his defined eyebrows. I looked again at his eyes, but still I couldn't make out the hazel color at all. In person, Sebastian's eyes only made him more intriguing than he already was, his eyes giving you the feeling that they saw *you*.

My eyes dropped from the top of the photo down to Sebastian's jacket. We'd gotten it together on an impromptu shopping trip down Michigan Avenue. The jacket had a few black zippers lining the tops of small flat pockets. I studied the pockets, trying to see if there were recent indents that would indicate what they'd held, if anything.

I focused on the right breast pocket. When we'd bought the jacket, the pocket had been plain, simple, which Sebastian liked, no overt logo or branding. But now something was there, some kind of patch? I leaned closer then, still unable to make out much of anything, I fiddled with Barbara's laptop until I found the zoom function.

"Huh," I said. I saw something gold-colored now on the pocket, gold in the shape of…what was it?

I leaned in. "Oh, my God!" I said suddenly, un-able to help the delighted tone.

I knew that Sebastian had absconded with one of Baxter's Superdog collars, claiming it was too ridicu-lous and saying, *we need to get some of these off the street.* And yet, there was a piece of it on his jacket. He must have cut a star off of the collar and had someone sew it onto the pocket. He and his mother had frequented the same dry cleaners for years— "the Greeks on Wrightwood," they fondly referred to them. Sebastian was a big fan of getting things tailored by the Greeks. They loved him.

And now here. He hadn't told me he'd done that. *So sweet,* I thought, over and over. So *sweet.*

I reached out to the laptop and lightly touched the part of the screen that showed the star, then moved my fingers to Sebastian's face.

"We're here," I said.

41

I called Barbara's sisters and waited until they arrived, then updated them with what little information I had. Barbara came downstairs, and they swarmed around her, hugging her, kissing her, murmuring comfort.

"Thank God you were here," one of them said, looking at me.

The rest looked over their shoulders, echoing, "Thank God."

One of them took me aside. "We've all seen the magazine," she said. "And we love you. We don't care what happened so many years ago."

"Thank you," I said. I smiled, finally feeling an emotion other than the generalized fear.

Watching Barbara and her sisters, though, gave me a whirl of sadness. I didn't have emotional reserves and support like they did. Not anymore. I'd thought I'd found a real companion in Gavin. I was wrong.

So I needed to create the reserves again. I saw that then. I suddenly remembered a therapist I saw after the arrest, a volunteer for the Amalie Project, who'd said, *You don't just get a community, you must find one and join one.*

The Amalie Project. Now that the news of my arrest was out, I no longer pushed away the memory. The Amalie Project. They took women in when no one else would. That's what most of the women said about it. Most had looked for answers elsewhere and for one reason or another been turned away. For me, I'd lucked into the project, having consulted and sought help from no one except the legal system.

I'd sought help from no one, certainly not my parents. I had a small part in their life, and I hadn't known how they would react. I hadn't wanted to risk being cut free.

But they'd found out. I had listed them as my emergency contacts, not because I'd believed they would be called for any reason. (I wasn't going to have any emergencies.) They'd been called by the program, accidentally, to confirm a follow-up on one of my appointments. I had already exited the program and was running fast toward a different life.

I could do little to convince them I didn't have a problem with drugs. That they never quite believed me just served to reinforce the feeling that they didn't know me. Did not want to look far enough inside.

But I saw now that the Amalie Project therapist

had been right about the need to create a community, rather than hoping or expecting one to arrive. I needed to cultivate friends, a support system.

I hugged Barbara on her porch before I left, both of us promising to reach out if we heard anything at all.

"I'm glad you were here," Barbara said, "for the last part of that life."

Strangely, I understood. She hadn't wanted her sisters to come yet—it would signal a turn toward the seriousness of the situation. She had wanted to sit on her front steps and feel normal for a bit, before she let everything and everybody sink in.

I nodded.

"I'm glad it was you," she said.

I reached out and squeezed her tighter. No one had ever said such a thing to me.

"What will you do now?" she said when we pulled apart.

The answer was already there, as if it was just waiting for the question to be spoken aloud.

"I'm going to call my parents."

42

A few hours later, a knock on the front door of my condo sent Baxter into a paroxysm of barks. Before the accident, I would have scolded him, but now it thrilled me to see his spirit.

The doorman was outside. "Flowers," he said. A large round white vase filled with blue hydrangeas. "These are the prettiest flowers I've ever seen. And I've seen a lot of flowers."

I smiled. They could only be from my parents, who had hydrangeas all over their property in the summer. Like the alchemists they were, they constantly played with the amount of aluminum they put in the soil to make the hydrangeas light blue, sea blue, palest purple, pink. Their property was a piece of art that they created together. Hydrangeas were their favorite, and had always been mine, too.

"We're on our way," the card read. "Hang in there! We love you."

I sat down on the couch, and I promptly cried. If

I accepted that moment as it was. I accepted that my ex-husband had been arrested in a country where anything could happen and that he had a very unsure future and it made me conflicted with emotion. I accepted that aside from his safety, there was nothing more I wanted than those blue flowers, that note from my parents. And so despite the situation, I felt grateful. They were coming! They were coming for me. And why? Because I had reached out. Because I had asked them to. They were despondent for Sebastian, who they very much cared for, but excited to be consulted. My dad had packed a bag for them (just one bag for the two of them) and they were in the car by the time my mom and I had finished our phone conversation. They'd gotten a flight from Buffalo. They would be here in a few hours.

I threw myself into getting the spare room ready. I moved artwork around the apartment so that the second bedroom had some of the most interesting pieces. I brought pillows from my bedroom that I knew they would like. All the while Baxter scampered around me, occasionally putting a ball at my feet to see if I would play. Instead we took a walk to a grocery store at Clark and Division. I clipped Baxter's leash to a rail with a few other dogs, who immediately moved in for a sniff and greet.

I bought fruit and wine and cheese, plus things to make my parents for dinner—chicken and pasta. I felt, in some ways, as though I was preparing for a fun weekend. My parents were coming to support me, to be with me, and I could not help but feel elated about that.

When the doorbell rang, I froze. I was only a few feet away, just in the kitchen, but suddenly I remembered what Barbara meant about the last moment of a previous life—holding on to a life because you knew that life was about to change.

Baxter was at the door, barking like a little madman, his spirits again cheering me.

When I opened my door, my parents were standing shoulder to shoulder, as they often were. My mother was a thin woman. She was of Scandinavian descent, and you could tell that, in part, by the minimalist way she dressed. In the winter she usually wore a feltlike coat in ivory, along with black riding pants, black riding boots. But now she sported her summer look, which was a slim, black cotton skirt to the floor, a white, short-sleeved shirt and a light blue scarf around her neck. My father, on the other hand, was a big man, unafraid to take up space. He let his belly grow from the cooking and baking he did. His hair, pushed back in a still-stylish manner, was now thick and white. My mom's hair was pixie cut and mousy-brown. Individually, they were vaguely interesting. Together, they were lightning, charisma, shine, sparkle.

They stood for a moment, both gazing at me, and then they rushed inside, arms around me. I felt what

Barbara must have with her sisters—comfort, release.

Eventually we sat at the table, my parent eschewing water or anything to eat.

"Have you heard news?" my dad said. "Since we were on the phone?"

"Poor Sebastian!" my mother said. "Can you imagine…?"

"Well, exactly," my father answered.

"It's…" my mom started.

"Disgraceful," my dad finished for her.

They often spoke in shorthand.

Darling, my mom might say over dinner, apropos of nothing apparent, but looking at my dad with questioning eyes that said, *Don't you need to…?*

No, my father would answer, without waiting for the question. *I took care of that already.* Later I would find out that they were discussing something as exciting as taking out the recycling.

A few minutes later, my mom might look up from her plate. *And did you…?*

I did. And the other thing, too.

My mother would give my father a sweet smile across the table.

I was always envious when I watched their brand of verbal Morse code, when I saw the love and the sparkle. And yet I was always grateful that, even if I didn't exactly share it, their brand of adoration existed. Sometimes I thought of one of my parents dying. And it scared me, not for me or the grief I would surely feel, but for whoever was left behind. My parents operated as a unit, always. What would happen when only one remained?

Right then my dad moved his hand to mine and covered it. He nodded, encouraging me to tell them.

"Beverly told us there's a video now in addition to the picture." I marveled at how *Beverly,* the name of the State Department lady, rolled off my tongue, as if she were a friend. I'd only spoken to her for about five minutes. She'd mostly wanted to introduce herself, since Barbara had told her she had shared information with me.

"A video?" my dad said.

I'd received a short email from Beverly just before they arrived. Video released of Hess and Baxter. We will send to Barbara, as our rules require next of kin.

"Can they use the Superdog attention to get some attention here?" my mom asked.

"That's what I've been wondering, too. Beverly says it would only confuse things right now." I stood. "I'll get my laptop and show you the photo." I stopped walking. "If you want to see it."

"Of course," my parents said in unison.

Of course. They were visual people.

"We want to be involved," my dad said.

"*If* we can help," my mother added. "Sometimes people have to help themselves." She nodded at me. "That's what you always told us."

I blinked fast. Baxter was at my feet. I held my arms open and let him jump into them, squeezing him for comfort.

"Mom, look…" I said.

"We saw the magazine," my father said. "About Billy. And you."

I flinched inwardly.

Almost as if he were miming me and Baxter, my dad stood then and opened his arms. I hesitated, then placed Baxter down and launched myself into his embrace.

My mother stood, too. They both hugged me.

"I saw Billy," I said. They both pulled back, eyes wide, and then we sat down.

Normally, my father would lead the conversation for them, be the one to ask the questions. But he was pissed off that Billy had rejected me all those years ago.

So my mom launched in instead, and I basked in her questions—"How did it feel to see him? How did the meeting come about? Was it difficult? Are you okay?"

Eventually, my father asked, "How is Billy's family?"

"He doesn't speak with Mick anymore. Other than that, I didn't have a chance to find out. I was talking with him when I got the news from Barb about Sebastian."

"Oh, honey," my mom said.

I felt comfort from them. I reveled in it.

But then something struck me. "It must be terribly embarrassing for you," I said, my face in my hands now, and it felt good to mimic a motion recently made by my mom. "This news of my arrest must have been terrible for your art careers."

"Bah!" my dad said dismissively.

My mother murmured her protests, and they told me, both of them told me, over and over and over that they loved me.

This time, for some reason, I believed them.

43

"If you die, what you want to say?"

The voice came from behind the camera, his English poor.

On the video, Sebastian and his photographer were sitting against the wall. They both looked very, very tired.

"Okay, then each say three persons to say when dead," the voice said, his glee evident. He sounded as if he were leading blissfully excited first-graders on their first pony ride. That pissed me off. And that surprised me. I didn't get mad often. I got disappointed, I got depressed, but not mad.

But that jackhole militant/police officer/whatever he was (Beverly had said they couldn't be sure of the group that had detained Sebastian) was joking about Sebastian dying? I flushed with rage. I turned my attention back to the video.

"Who you want to know when you die?" The man's voice had gotten some composure, his English improving. He zoomed the camera toward the photographer, next to Sebastian. The photographer named Baxter. "Three people."

I was sitting in Barbara's kitchen again, the morning after my parents arrived. They were still asleep at my place. I reached down for Baxy and put him on my lap.

On the video, the photographer named Baxter spoke. "Lauren Baxter. Jackson Dilly. Anthony Baxter."

"Say three people," the delighted voice said, turning the camera on Sebastian. In the same clothes, squatting now as if very comfortable with the position.

Sebastian cleared his throat. "Jessica Champlin," he said.

I gasped.

"Barbara Hess," he said. "And Baxter Hess."

I immediately burst into tears—a bouquet of droplets falling onto Baxter's soft head, the tears representing stress, fear, confusion and also, right at that moment, happiness and love.

Sebastian had thought I could deal with it. He'd thought that Baxy and I could deal with the dangerous ramifications of his job. Now he wanted me to be his...well, his first of kin.

I walked to the front door and opened it. Barbara was outside again—on the porch, her arms between her legs, looking to the street, but with a vacant stare.

She was usually the busiest of women, especially when something had to do with her kids.

I said her name. Slowly, she turned around, looked at me.

"Barb, where are your sisters?"

"One is upstairs. The others are coming back in an hour."

"Good."

"Sebastian…" She shook her head.

"You haven't watched the video yet?"

"No. I can't. But I want to know what's in it."

I took a breath and then I told her. I told her the question they had been asked. "He lists me, you and…" I gave a soft laugh. "And Baxter. The dog Baxter, not Bill the photographer."

That made her smile minutely, but then the question must have hit her, her expression returning to one so bleak, so tired.

I sat on the steps and touched her hand. "It's going to be fine."

She looked at me, shocked. "*You* know it's not."

"I know?"

"You were always the one who said his job could end his life."

I had never said as much to Barbara. Sebastian must have told her I'd said it to him.

"And you were right!" She sounded shrill.

"I'm not right. I wasn't."

"You were."

Sebastian's mom was in her early sixties but could usually pass for a decade younger. Now she appeared aged somehow. Weak. Diminished.

"And he risked himself for what?" she said. "To report on the stories that needed to be told? Blah, blah." Barb sucked in air and seemed to crumple a little with the exhale.

When she spoke again, her voice was a bitter whisper. "You were right."

44

What a strange, strange world mine had become. Strang*er,* I suppose I should say.

I walked Baxter through Lincoln Park in a light summer rain. Baxter liked the rain because he could trot about, plunge into puddles, then stop and shake off the water and do it again. I liked it because there was no one around, and I could consider what a strange, strange world mine had become.

My parents, who I'd rarely seen for years, were ensconced in my apartment (all of us happily, comfortably, *strange*ly). Meanwhile, my ex-husband Billy was in town staying at a lux hotel, *Just in case you need anything at all,* he had said more than once, texted more than once.

In talking with him, what I realized I needed most from Billy was his ear. Not his musical ear, but his listening one. I talked to him about Sebastian, mostly telling him the story of how Sebastian and I had met, where we'd lived, the places we had traveled and why we'd broken up. Then I would start over, and Billy kept listening, asking different questions each time, and I wasn't even embarrassed, and I would find side angles to our story that I'd forgotten.

I was relieved to relive it. And it kept my mind far away from the magazine article and my full voice mail and multitudes of texts and emails. None of that mattered now. In that way, I was grateful for the situation with Sebastian—it had given perspective to my past.

"And I'm realizing something," I told Billy now on the phone. "What I'm realizing is that I want to keep it alive. Sebastian and me."

"But you don't want to keep us alive?" Billy said, gesturing between us.

"Us as friends, I do. I'm grateful for you."

"What about as something more than friends?"

I thought of Billy, of his green eyes and dirty-blond hair. He always looked so adorable to me, since I'd first known him.

"It's too long dead," I told him.

He blew out a puff of air, as if he'd been holding it until he got my answer. But then he said, "I understand."

I was so thankful then to have Billy. Repairing us in that way made my feelings about the magazine article, my past, come into more perspective, get placed in the proper level of my present.

And right then, something bobbed into my consciousness, something broke through a tiny crack in the shell I wore, one that held the decisions I'd made about Sebastian, the conclusions, the shading of the truth. And the thought was this—*Sebastian loves me unconditionally.*

The truth of that statement kept breaking over me, rushing through the crack, light seeping into dark.

I told Billy about that, too. "Well, that's good, right?" he asked.

"I'm not sure." In fact, I wasn't sure I could handle the intensity of the emotion.

"Billy," I had said upon feeling the swell, the rush, "I'll call you back."

I turned and headed back home, to my parents, walking Bax through the rain.

After a minute, I let Baxter's leash drop, let him bound ahead of me on the wet path.

Sebastian *had always* loved me. I knew that. I'd always known that basic fact, but when we were together I thought he hadn't loved me enough— evidenced by his unwillingness to change the conditions of his job. He always said he would try—that he wouldn't take so many overseas assignments, that he would work in the newsroom, would start to take a managing role. And he did try a few times, particularly when we moved to Chicago, but in the end the job won. That's what I'd thought.

I watched Baxter pawing at the mud, as if he'd found something stuck there.

"Bax, stop!" I said. But his DNA digging instincts must have kicked in, because he started frantically burrowing, his butt in the air, mud flying behind him from between his legs.

"Baxter, stop!" I walked toward him fast, but he was lost in that motion, in that mud.

That's what I do, too. I get lost.

My instincts were to assume people didn't love me, or didn't love me enough. I'd dig and dig, looking around for the evidence, and I kept finding it. Or so I thought. But maybe I was just unable to stop my re-action. Because a lack of love wasn't what I had, not with my parents, not with Billy, and not, I realized now, with Sebastian. His love *was* unconditional, despite what he could or could not do at my request.

"Baxter!" I said.

Finally, my voice had penetrated the instinctive behavior. His brown eyes were big, a little startled-looking. He glanced around, like, *What? What did I do?*

"Come!" I said, pointing to the ground. He listened then, he dodged to me. I bent, kissing his wet nose and forehead. He looked up at me, thumping his tail, seeming so happy. I couldn't help but hug him, mud or not.

I hugged Baxter tighter. I let other thoughts—new and old—about Sebastian enter my mind. I didn't bat any away. I didn't look away. And then another thought, a memory really, came back.

It was of a brunch Sebastian and I once had in New York. On the Upper West Side, a few blocks from my apartment. It had been dumping rain, and so we'd gone inside and tucked into a booth and stayed for hours. And in answer to my questions, Sebastian had talked about his job.

The table was covered with a checkered tablecloth, I remember, because Sebastian said it reminded him of a restaurant in France. And as if we were in Europe, we ordered menu items slowly, and then shared them.

When I asked Sebastian what he liked most about his job, he thought for a long time.

"You know what I like?" he said. "I like when I know something for certain and yet the government in that country denies the piece of information."

"Why would you like that?"

"Because I've found the truth."

"And now you're going to fight a government to expose it?"

"Not fight, necessarily. Sometimes the government is misleading you intentionally." The waiter put down an omelet with porcini mushrooms. Sebastian's passion made him ignore it, lean over it to keep talking. "Sometimes they just don't know the situation as well as a journalist who has special sources different from the government."

"Doesn't that scare you?" I asked. "You're not

in politics, but you're dealing with foreign govern-
ments. *And* you might know more than they do?"

"Yeah, sometimes." With that simple admission
he leaned back, his eyes seeming to go somewhere
for a minute. "And you're dealing with people. Real
people." He picked up his fork and used it to slice
off some omelet. "It's the people, of course, who
break your heart."

It wasn't just a sad statement; he said it with such
forlorn emotion I wanted to jump on his lap and hug
him and kiss his cheek and tell him all would be
okay. "I take it that happened to you on the job," I
said. "Heartbreak?"

"Sure, lots of times. You develop a relationship
with them, and they happen to live in a war-torn
country, so naturally some will die young and violently. It's a fact."

"Not a fun one," I said.

"No." He sighed. "And it's not just the people you
meet. It could be one of us who gets killed."

"Us?"

He only gave a slight nod, not saying anything.

I stayed silent, wanting him to talk, but afraid to
break the moment. It seemed to me then that we were
treading into new territory for us, territory Sebastian hadn't yet shared. And I wanted to understand
his job better so I could try and get on board with it.
I also wanted to simply share, to know.

"One of my friends…" Sebastian said. "A journalist." He paused. "He was kidnapped by rebels, and they cut off his hand. Can you imagine?"

"Why?"

"They regretted giving him information. They decided he might give it to the wrong people. It was a symbolic act."

"Horrific," I said. Just one word. I could think of no others.

He nodded. "Once that happened, he wasn't just a witness anymore. He was a witness *and* a participant." Another pause. "It's a hard place to be."

Now the rain had stopped momentarily, but Baxter was still very wet. I put him on the ground, then stood and turned for home.

But I kept thinking of that brunch. Of the way Sebastian spoke about being a witness and a participant. The more I thought about it, something nudged my subconscious. I thought harder about that brunch, but all I could remember was that Sebastian didn't talk much the rest of the time. I filled in the silence, waiting for what I'd heard to settle. I'm not sure that it ever did. I never entirely understood him.

And now it only raised questions. A lot of them.

I took out my phone and called the State Department.

45

Beverly didn't answer right away, but she called me back within five minutes. "You saw it?" she said. "The video?"

"Yeah, I watched it at Barb's."

"I know that must have been hard," Beverly said. "To hear the questions about death."

"Yeah, but it was nice to be mentioned."

We both chuckled lightly. I was still handling it.

"You've been divorced for a few years, right?" Beverly asked.

"Yes." I got a flash of being in front of the judge to finalize our divorce. I felt a slice in the gut like I always did when I thought of standing at that bench, saying the words that would end us—*experienced and will continue to experience irreconcilable differences.*

But it was more painful to remember the divorce than usual. Now that Sebastian was…God knows where.

I wondered what else Beverly knew about me and Sebastian. Did she know about my drug arrest, my marriage to Billy? Of course she did. Even if the story hadn't been in the magazine Gavin worked for (and the subsequent others), I knew that if celeb mags or a hack like Gavin could find my information, the State Department would find out much more. Thankfully, there was nothing else.

"Beverly, I have some questions," I said. Baxter and I got to North Avenue, and he started pulling to the right. He wanted to go to the dog park.

"Baxter, no," I said, tugging him toward the house.

He stopped and eyed me, trying mentally to entice me into taking him.

He must have realized I wouldn't cave. He gave a grand shake from head to butt, shaking off the walk and a hell of a lot of mud. Some landed on my clothes, but I didn't care. I was too focused on the questions.

"Can you tell me why this situation with Sebastian hasn't been in the media?" I asked Beverly. "I mean, I'm glad, I guess. But I don't understand why." I was beginning to sense I didn't understand a lot.

"They still haven't told the media yet. That's good."

"'They' meaning the authorities in Libya?"

"Right."

"Who are these authorities?"

I stopped Baxter and pulled a small pad of paper from my pocket. It was one of Sebastian's notepads that I occasionally still found at my house. I'd started carrying it around since he was taken, needing to record notes, but also liking the connection to him, feeling for the first time some glimpse into Sebastian's professional mind, the one that needed to jot down the most random of things, because sometimes they "assembled." That's how Sebastian had explained it to me. Sometimes the scraps of information and names and thoughts gathered into some thing cohesive.

"What do you mean?" Beverly said.

"Well, are these local authorities who have him? Are we talking the police station from a small town or province? Is he even at a police station? Did they get in an accident? Or did someone mistakenly think they stole something?"

Beverly was quiet.

"Or is it a higher authority, a government or whatever, that's higher up?" I asked. "Is it federal in nature?"

"We hope to gather that information shortly from our various sources of intel."

It all sounded so routine, so clean—gather that information… Various sources of intel…

"Remind me how we first knew about the photo?" I liked the word *we*.

"Good question. We got a call from someone on

the ground that a reporter and photographer hadn't returned to their hotel rooms. We put the word out and one of our sources received that picture anonymously."

"Via email?"

"Correct."

"Can we track the email?"

"We're trying."

"And the video? How did we get that?"

"The government sent it to us."

"But you don't know what government?"

Silence.

"And what about *our* government?" I asked, my voice getting a little louder. "What are we doing to get these guys free? What are you doing?"

"This is frustrating, Jessica, but as I'm sure you know when someone gets arrested in another country, that person is entirely subject to the laws of that country or state, even if they differ significantly from ours."

"Right. But the question remains—what are you doing?"

"We're monitoring the state of the country now, and their stance regarding the United States."

"Which is?" I asked.

"We're collecting information on that. And we'll monitor conditions of the location they're being held."

"When you find out where that is."

"Right."

"Or whenever you decide to tell us." I couldn't help but sound bitter. Not being able to do anything was beginning to make me itchy.

"Jessica," Beverly said, "I'm trying. I really am. I want to share everything with you, but information has to be confirmed. And to be honest, technically I shouldn't be talking directly to you. You're not married to Sebastian anymore."

I stopped on State Street. Baxter tugged at the leash, already looking forward to a treat at home, I supposed. "So why have you done it? Why have you shared with me?"

"Because I saw that video. I saw it sooner than you did, and I heard him say your name, and your dog's name. And it was clear."

"What was clear?"

"A few things. But mostly that he wanted you to know."

My body seemed to thump at those words. I plainly felt my heartbeat near my chest, sending blood to the rest of my body.

"What's the next step?" I asked. "Traditionally."

"There are a number of things that could happen—release, contact from the government, the government allowing the guys to contact us, formal charges, disclosure of charges… I could go on and on."

"What about doing our own media?" I said. "We haven't talked about Baxter."

When she said nothing again, I asked. "You know about the dog Sebastian and I share? Baxter?"

"Yes, Superdog. Of course. We've known from the beginning."

"Right." I kept walking. "And you've known since the beginning of what?"

A minute pause. "This situation," she said vaguely.

"Right," I said again, frustrated. "Well, did you consider whether that would help the situation? I mean is there any way we could work that? Tell the media that the dad of Superdog is missing overseas." It sounded silly to my own ears.

"Yes, briefly. But that type of news coverage is primarily celebrity in nature, and that is highly volatile in terms of being able to control your message."

"What is our message?"

"Jessica, I'll get more information soon," she said. "I'm sure. And I'll call you as soon as I do."

I was still frustrated by what she was holding back.

We both fell quiet for a moment. Then I said, "Thanks." Because what else could I say?

46

I called Billy on the walk home. "Would you want to meet my parents again?"

"Sure." No pause before that word.

"Are you still in Chicago?"

"Yeah. I'm not leaving until you want me to."

"Don't you have events, concerts? Your kid? Doesn't your manager want to kill you?" I remembered when I knew his manager, remembered when I knew exactly what was on Billy's schedule. The strangeness of it all struck again, the fact that I had been so squarely in someone's life and now was so far from it.

We were coming closer, though, in a deep friendship kind of way.

"I'm handling it," he said. "Don't worry."

I was glad for him, then. Billy used to struggle with making decisions about his schedule, his work, his life. He let the manager or Mick make decisions for him.

"Meet me at my place?" I asked. "My parents are there."

"Of course," he said, again with no pause, no question. He knew my father wasn't a fan of his anymore, but he didn't mention it. And the conversation made me wonder, again, why I didn't ask for help more often.

Thirty minutes later the doorman called to tell me Billy was on his way up from the lobby.

I picked Baxter up again. This time he was wrapped in a towel. My mother had insisted on giving him a bath.

I turned to my parents, who were seated at the kitchen table in the bay window. "You sure you guys are okay with this?"

"Yes," they said in unison.

My mom wore a black skirt and white blouse with a lavender scarf around her neck. My dad was in a blue shirt, which made his tan and his white hair stand out more. He had rolled up the sleeves as if ready for work. My parents had helped me as much as they could. Still, I knew they must be craving their art or at least some activity.

"Well, I know we haven't talked about that time in a while." *That time I was arrested.* "But you're okay?"

"Billy was responsible," my dad said. "But we'll overlook it."

"No, he wasn't responsible. If anything it was Mick, but ultimately it's my responsibility only."

They nodded. They'd never been able to get their heads around why someone who wasn't a drug user would buy drugs.

I felt a flutter of anticipation, and I could feel my parents do so, as well.

A knock on the door sent Baxter flying from my arms, barking madly.

When I opened the door, Billy kissed me chastely on the cheek and then immediately bent down. Baxter flew into his arms and began licking his face, apparently having made the snap doggy judgment that, *This here is a dog person.* Their hair was the same color, I noticed. If Baxter was my kid he looked more like Billy than Sebastian.

"Billy McGowan," my mom said, crossing the kitchen. My dad stood but stayed near the table.

They shook hands, then my mom hugged him while my father scowled nearby.

When they pulled apart after the brief hug, I suddenly felt, *Whoa.* A weird moment was upon us. The awkwardness of the situation was clear, made me wonder if I'd been too hasty in pulling together the two parties who had been providing me the most support. I didn't know if my dad would ever forgive.

But then my dad held his hand out and moved forward, and Billy was grasping it and then they embraced, too.

"I'm sorry, sir," Billy said. "I'm very sorry I didn't take care of her."

My dad hugged him tighter, and the room felt strangely, suddenly comfortable.

"You look wonderful," Billy said to my mom, and I heard his voice as if he were fourteen. The memory felt that fresh.

My mom smiled at him, just the way she used to.

I directed everyone to the bay window and the table. I had pulled out some crackers and hummus, which I set on the table now. I made offers of water or iced tea.

Billy looked at his watch. It was nearly 5:00 p.m. "Do you have a beer?"

"Amen," my father said.

Billy and my dad drank beers, while my mom and I had iced tea. I led the talk round to Sebastian. Then I let my other ex-husband fuel our discussion.

"I feel like I need to brainstorm about Sebastian being kidnapped," I told them. "And I'd like your help. The State Department says they've considered everything and that they understand this type of situation, but I want to do anything I can, anything we can."

"Amen," my father said again, although he never went to church.

I told them about the growing number of questions I had and the frustrating phone call with Beverly. I told them how I wondered if they should be using the Superdog story to fuel some movement.

"Well, what about calling our legislators first?" my mother offered.

"Good idea," my father said. He pointed out that I was in Illinois, they were in New York, and Billy had three homes but spent most of his time in Huntington Beach—we had more than a few politicians we could call.

I brought out my laptop, and we researched legislators' contact numbers. We each sent out a number of emails, made phone calls to legislative offices. None of them were in session, we were told, but they all had assistants who were surprisingly willing to listen.

We'd decided not to mention Superdog yet and only tell them of Sebastian's arrest, that we were family and friends looking for information and help.

"Now what?" my mom said a few hours later. "What else can we do?" She was animated in a way I hadn't seen often, and it thrilled me.

We fell silent, each of us thinking.

"I know someone in Jordan," Billy said.

"Someone from Jordan, the country?" I said.

"Yeah. I did this party overseas," Billy said, "and I met some people from Jordan."

"Okay." I kept myself from asking, *How is that useful?* because I saw in his hesitant expression that Billy McGowan was bashful. No one else would notice such a thing, except maybe his family, and me. I had been the recipient of that bashfulness (the original version of it), starting when I was fourteen. "Who do you know in Jordan?"

"Well, someone high up. I mean…" He shrugged. "They have a parliament and everything, but you know… I met the royal family."

"Wow," I said. The McGowans of yore, the ones I'd known, may have met a mayor or two passing through towns, but that was it. "Does that help us here?"

"Libya is nearby—they may have connections with people there. So I'm wondering if they can help, if I had someone call them. My manager, maybe."

"Why not you?" my mom said. "Wouldn't they be more likely to take a call from Billy McGowan?"

"Maybe we should wait for the government to reach out?" I said. Yet I said it weakly, almost as though I was required to say it. But really I was both scared and thrilled with the thought of taking matters into our own hands.

"I don't know how it could hurt if Billy just said hello and felt out the situation," my dad said.

"I can be delicate," Billy said. I saw a yearning in him. Was it a need to help me? Or was he at a place in his life where he needed this kind of thing, something different? "I understand that there are politically sensitive considerations." Billy sounded so adult. Sometimes it was hard to speed-age him from fourteen to now.

I pulled my laptop to me. "Let's see what time it is there." I ran a search. "Three o'clock in the morning in Amman."

Billy started scrolling through his phone. "I can text the guy who takes care of the prince. He'll get the message when he gets up."

My mom scooted closer to Billy.

"Okay," Billy said, as if he needed momentum. He typed on his phone, holding it out a little so my mom could see over his shoulder. "I just asked him to give me a call. Now, what else?"

47

A few hours later we had rounded through as many possibilities as we could think of to help Sebastian, weighing each, debating whether I should let Beverly know about our brainstorming. It had been exhausting.

"Holy shit," Billy said, looking at his phone.

"I know," I said. "It's past nine."

My dad sipped the rest of his beer and plunked it on the table. "Off to bed." He grinned at Billy. They were each four beers deep. The drinks seemed to bond them.

Billy's phone rang then. "Wow," he said, still looking at the phone.

Then he added, "Holy shit," again, then looked up at my mom. "Sorry about the swearing."

"I've heard such language, Billy."

"What is it?" I asked.

Billy responded by quickly standing. "Hello? This is Billy McGowan." He raised his eyebrows at me.

It's him, he mouthed, and I knew it wasn't just a congressman. I felt happy that even Billy McGowan could be awed at the thought of royalty.

"Yes, yes," he said after listening for a minute.

He pointed toward the hallway and I nodded. When he walked that way, I got a flash of Gavin taking a phone to that hall to talk privately, and of the hell that transpired thereafter.

I shook the thought away.

Billy launched into what sounded like brief small talk before I could no longer hear him.

Ten minutes later he came down the hall and into the kitchen again. "They know Superdog."

As if on cue, Baxter leaped into my lap.

"What do you mean?" I said.

"I told them I was calling about two reporters who'd been detained or arrested in Libya, and as part of the background I told them Sebastian was part owner of this dog that's been in some videos. Then he told me that one of the smaller kids in the family was a huge fan of Superdog."

"C'mon," I said, scratching Baxter's head.

"I'm serious. He offered to use it to bring it up to the family and see what they know about the situation with Libya."

His phone rang again.

"Yes," he said, answering. "Uh-huh, uh-huh. Well, that would be great. Thank you."

He turned to us. "They are going to reach out and see what they can find."

"Perfect," my mom said.

"Wait a sec," I said. "This is exciting, but I don't want to cause any trouble." I stood. "Let me call Beverly."

"Okay, hold on," Beverly said when I called her and told her the basics. "Run this by me again."

I wondered what she looked like, this faceless Beverly.

Once again, I told her that Billy knew the Jordanians and had contacted them, and they knew Superdog, and they offered to assist if needed.

"We need to slow down here," she said.

"I don't know how we can slow down. We're not even moving."

"We are. And there's no reason to have an ex-wife talking to some *rock musician*…" she said this derisively "…who then calls a Middle Eastern *prince* and discusses a *dog video.*"

Now that she said it, it did sound ridiculous. But if Baxter's fame could be used for anything, it should be to bring Sebastian back. And Billy was more than willing to use his own fame.

"I know I'm not married to Sebastian anymore," I said, "but I want to help. His mom, Barb, is having a hard time dealing, and his brother lives in Europe. I want to be the point person here. And you saw the video…" I left unsaid, *Sebastian would want me to know.* "And you know about the Superdog video. You know how much attention we got from that. Hell, I got a whole business from that, which I've totally been ignoring because of this situation."

I had texted Toni earlier and told her to put a banner on the I'd Rather Sleep with the Dog website that said, *Due to high demand, we are operating at a slower than usual pace. Please be patient and check back with us if needed.*

According to Toni, people had checked in by email, but most assumed that the delays were due to Baxter's recovery and were completely understanding. In fact, sales had increased.

"What if I can get a phone call?" Beverly said on the phone now.

"A phone call," I repeated. "From whom? To whom?"

"What if I can get them to call us, and let you talk to Sebastian?"

"If you could do that, why wouldn't you have offered that sooner?" I failed to hide my annoyance.

"We are making gains," she said. "And we are able to do that now. This pace is somewhat standard in such a situation."

"What situation is that?" Again, annoyance. "You keep talking about gains and plans and intel and gathering, but I don't know that it's gotten us anywhere! I don't understand why it's so amorphous, why there aren't more details, more information, and I can only conclude that you can't share it with me for some reason."

I paused to let her protest. She didn't.

"So," I said, "I think our families need to make efforts on our end. We already emailed our legislators."

"You what?"

I told her about contacting senators and congress-persons in Illinois, New York and California.

"Okay," she said, voice businesslike and a little louder. "Please *do not* do that anymore. Please stop."

"Why?"

A sigh. "Jessica, give me until tomorrow," she said.

"Give you until tomorrow for what?"

"I'll call you then," she said. "Give me until then before you do anything else."

"Do you want them to call your cell?" Beverly said.

The previous night, I'd said good-night to my parents and Billy, and I'd gone to bed with Baxter. I was still in bed when Beverly called. In that time Beverly had gotten something done. Maybe I'd been too harsh to judge her.

"You're going to have Sebastian call me?" I said finally. "Or the people who are keeping him are going to call me?"

"Both. They will call you and let you talk to Sebastian."

"Wow. Great." It helped, apparently, to take matters into your own hands, and especially when you had Superdog on board. I was still handling the situation. Again, I saw that I'd been wrong when I told Sebastian I couldn't handle his job and the consequences. "I'd like them to call on my cell phone."

"I'm not sure if it will be tonight, their time, or tomorrow," Beverly said

I wasn't exactly sure what she meant, and I was about to say I didn't know if I wanted to wait until tomorrow, but Beverly spoke more quickly.

"Jess, we're going to have to explain something to you before you talk to him."

Why did that sound ominous? I sat up in bed, causing Baxter to yawn and stretch.

"Who is 'we'?" I said, shrugging on a light robe. Not the first time I'd asked that question.

"I'm about to explain that," Beverly said.

"So, you're going to tell me something via the State Department or some other organization?" Why couldn't I just shut up? I stood and paced around my bed, having a random recollection of buying that bed with Sebastian at a place on Diversey Avenue. "Beverly, I don't want to be ungrateful, but this situation is just getting more confusing."

"I know. That's why I got authorization to tell you."

"Tell me…" I stopped, sensing the tide changing.

Baxter, who had been trailing me, sat and looked up at me, expectant.

"Jess, Sebastian is part of a government organization, in addition to being a reporter. Or he has been, off and on."

"What do you mean?" I tried to gather what she'd said. "Sebastian works undercover or something?"

"Sometimes. As I mentioned, he is a journalist, always has been. But sometimes, as part of his duties as a journalist, he also collects intel for us."

"'Us,' as in…"

Finally, she spoke. "The CIA."

48

My bedroom felt as if it were fuzzing in front of me.

I had been bowled into silence. I felt for the wall and leaned back. I had no idea how long I'd been there, holding the phone, trying to process Beverly's words.

Baxter came closer to me and cocked his face up to mine.

"How long has this been going on?" I asked. "How long has he been working with you?"

My mind was assimilating. If I had to guess right then, I would have said that she would probably say, "A few years." (Such as during the few years Sebastian and I had been apart.)

"Since before you met him."

I slid to the floor. Baxter climbed on my lap.

Before you met him.

"He quit when you got engaged," she said. It was clear she knew exactly when our engagement had happened, when everything had happened in our lives.

"Okay…" I said, because although I wasn't fully understanding, I didn't want her to stop talking.

"But he agreed to come back sometime after you moved to Chicago."

For the first year Sebastian and I were in Chicago, he had spent time at home and in the office of the local paper where he'd taken a job. But after about a year, his travel had picked up, as had his assignments for his old paper in New York.

"Now it seems like Sebastian is making an effort to…uh…to get out again," Beverly said. "That's why he's in this situation."

"What do you mean?"

"He admitted to a source—in a very up-front way, so that word of his admission would travel—that he had obtained some dangerous information. That's why he was arrested."

Again, I kept thinking how Sebastian had a life going on without me, just like Billy McGowan had. But instead of disappointing me or hurting me, that knowledge was consoling because it explained Sebastian and his behavior at the time. I hadn't caused it. A lack of love had not caused it.

"You think Sebastian purposefully admitted to having some information, knowing you would find out?" I asked.

"Correct. And we think he did that so that he could get out of the CIA."

I thought about one night when Sebastian had been on a story for three weeks, when I'd gone through his home computer, looking for evidence of where he might be.

That night I sat down at Sebastian's desk in our office, something I rarely did, consumed by a need to know something, anything. I pulled out his checkbook, then remembered he didn't write checks. He paid everything online. I looked around the room. Sebastian and I had initially envisioned working together in here, swinging around to face each other to run something by one another.

I'd realized eventually that I was the one who'd envisioned us working that way. Sebastian had merely gone along with my vision. Because soon he was often at the paper, using the newsroom, accessing their archives. I didn't blame him. Being in the newsroom put him in the action.

However, Sebastian had been preparing for his trip a fair amount by using the home computer. Surely it would hold some answers. I'd felt, for some reason, that if I knew where he was, that knowledge might calm me.

The computer had asked for a pass code.

I'd typed in his childhood address. *Incorrect login!* the computer had said.

I'd tried his mom's maiden name, his first pet,

adding the numbers for his grandfather's birthday, which he had told me he often tacked on to passwords. *Incorrect login!* the computer had said again.

I'd tried other things, other permutations. *Incorrect login! Incorrect login!*

I'd begun to despise the invention of the exclamation mark.

Finally, a last shot, I'd put in my name with his grandfather's birthday. Nothing.

I had sat back then. It wasn't so strange that I couldn't decipher his passwords, but I'd had an inkling then that Sebastian wasn't everything he said he was. He had other parts of him.

I was right, I saw now. I just hadn't realized the extent of those parts.

"How would confessing to information help him get out of the CIA?" I said to Beverly now.

"The source he confessed to is low-level. So the government isn't sure they believe the source. Sebastian would know that there would be a question about him. He knew he would likely get picked up. But he would also know that the government in Libya doesn't want to piss off our government. So that's why we've had some cooperation."

"That's why you got the photo and video?"

"Yes."

"And that's why they're going to let him call me?"

"Yes."

"Will they be on the line or whatever? Will they be listening?"

"Yeah." I heard the sound of a keyboard. "Hold on." Some more silence. "Okay, I just got word, they won't just be listening. They'll be watching, too. This is going to be a video call." She mentioned the software that I could get as an app on my phone.

"I already have it," I told her.

"Good." She paused.

I got a flicker of anticipation. "Is there anything I should say? Or not say?" *Please don't let me screw up when Sebastian's life is at stake.*

But I could almost hear my ex-husband's reply. *You can handle it.*

"Yes," Beverly said. "Just please do not reference the conversation we had tonight. In any way."

"Got it," I said.

49

Sebastian's face—his sweet, sweet face—appeared on my screen.

The phone had bleated an alert for an incoming video call. When I tapped on the icon, it seemed interminable before I actually saw a picture.

And then Sebastian.

"Hi, honey," he said.

I gulped. Felt as if I wanted to cry. "How are you?"

"I'm okay."

"You are?"

"Yeah."

I searched his face for fear, for any other emotion, since he likely felt he couldn't tell me, didn't want to admit apprehension. But he was too hard to read emotionally. He didn't look much different except that he looked thin and like he was growing a slight beard.

"How's Baxter?" he asked.

I picked Baxter up with my free hand, scooping him around his chest and raising him to my face.

"Dogger!" Sebastian said, but he said it weakly.

We talked about Baxter and how he was doing after his accident. I told him about how he was no longer off balance when he went to catch a ball.

"He's fine now," I said. "Absolutely fine."

"Great."

We discussed our dog like we had any other time since our divorce, and for a moment I forgot the situation we were in. But then Sebastian looked over his shoulder. I couldn't see what was behind him, except something white, like someone had put up a white sheet.

He turned back to face the screen. "God, I want so badly to be there."

I put Baxter down. Standing from the chair in my bedroom, I moved to the window. I opened it and held the phone out, showing Sebastian the view from our bedroom.

"Oh, God," I heard Sebastian say again. "God, Jess…"

I turned the phone back to my face. I wasn't sure how much time we had. I didn't want to leave anything unsaid. "Sebastian, I know this isn't really important now, but maybe…well, maybe it is. Maybe it will be important going forward."

He nodded.

"What I have to tell you is that I was married before. I was married when I was young."

He nodded again.

"You know the McGowan Brothers band," I said. "I was married to the youngest. Billy McGowan. And I was arrested during that time. For drugs."

There. It was out.

Sebastian remained quiet for a while, seemingly searching for words.

"I'm sorry to drop this on you now," I said. "It's silly, I guess. It doesn't matter."

"You were married," he said, finally speaking. "Why didn't you tell me that?"

I said nothing for a moment. It seemed misguided now that I hadn't told him about it. It seemed misguided that I hadn't been up-front and honest with Sebastian about everything. Maybe he would have confided in me about the double life he led professionally. Who knows, maybe such honesty would have saved our marriage. Or maybe Gavin had been right and the information would cause Sebastian to turn away for good.

"I guess I didn't tell you," I finally said, "because my marriage ended with me being arrested. I was embarrassed, mortified."

"Jess, don't say that." His expression softened. It seemed as if he were looking directly into my eyes. For a minute, I felt him. Right there.

"I knew," he said.

I blinked, returning my eyes and mind to the fact that I was in my bedroom with our dog, while Sebastian was in custody in another country. "You knew…"

"I knew about your marriage and I knew about the drug stuff."

"Oh." It struck me then. "Oh, you knew because you're…"

He threw a glance over his shoulder, nodded, gave me a pointed stare through the phone with a look that said, *Don't say anything else.*

"I love you, Jess," Sebastian said.

I felt a catch in my throat.

"Always have," he said.

I gulped, then opened my mouth to respond, but it didn't matter. Because the screen went black. Sebastian was gone again.

50

The next two days were the longest I have ever spent in my life. Even longer than those two days I spent in custody after I was arrested. I was lucky to not have gotten jail time. Now I almost wished I had. Maybe I would be better at waiting.

Mostly I sat with a book in my hands but not reading. I did it for Baxter, so he could sit at my feet and take a nap. Because whenever I was nervous, he became skittish. I wanted him to feel okay.

Of course, what I wanted most of all, I had no control over—Sebastian's safety.

My parents stayed with me, waited on me. They made me give up my cell phone sometimes for them to watch, and they made me try to sleep.

Billy was around some of those days, too. But I can't really recall if we had any conversations.

Mostly, I sat, book in hand, and thought about how I now understood that Sebastian had loved me in the past, even knowing my secrets and knowing

I wasn't sharing them with him. And he loved me now. He always had.

It was five in the afternoon when my father knocked on the door.

"Come in," I called.

He stepped inside. I looked up at him. So did Baxter. His eyes were big, excited.

I put my book down.

"Jess," he said. Then again, "Jess." He held up my cell phone.

"Yeah?" My voice creaked. I cleared my throat, tried to clear the fear coating it.

"He's out," my dad said. "They released him."

51

I was sitting just beyond the Welcome to Chicago sign at the airport when Sebastian came through customs, through the door and back into my life.

After we were notified when he would be home, I'd asked Barb if I could be the one to greet Sebastian, as long as I dropped him off at her house after. She'd reluctantly, but kindly, agreed.

His partner had returned on a separate flight, so Sebastian came through the door alone.

He smiled when he saw me. He walked toward me, but he was stopped by a young guy rushing into the arms of older men wearing turbans, all of them exclaiming with joy.

Next to me, a Mexican family spotted their relative or friend, and started waving and speaking loudly in Spanish.

Sebastian made his way around the first group, and then the second, and then he reached me. We hugged. Then harder. And then he picked me up and squeezed me to his chest, and I wanted so badly to kiss him.

After a minute, I said in his ear, "Welcome back." I meant, *Welcome back to our life, if you want it.*

"Thanks." He stared into my eyes and he grinned big, but I couldn't tell what he was thinking. "Thanks." He set me down, but we kept hugging.

"Are you feeling okay?" I asked.

"Fine."

"Are you hungry?"

"I got upgraded on the flight, and I pretty much ate the whole way."

I gestured toward the wall of windows that faced the arrivals area. "I got a town car," I said. "But maybe we can talk here for a minute, before we get back into everything." *Back into the world.* Whether it would be our world, I didn't know. But either way I wanted to have everything up front, nothing hiding in the corners of us.

He pulled me by my hand to a bench near a huge plate glass window. Outside, it was brilliantly sunny, and flags from every country whipped in the breeze.

"You can ask me anything, Jess," he said.

"Yeah?"

"I want to talk about it. And they've finally allowed me that with you. I'm ready, too." He scanned the crowd. "Just give me a minute to take everything in."

"Of course," I said. "Of course."

As his eyes searched for something, he spoke. "What have you been thinking about since we talked? While I was there?"

"Well…" I tried to review the chaotic thoughts that had coursed through my mind. "I have been wondering when you knew. About my being married, and my arrest."

"I found out after we got engaged. I hadn't told them I was proposing. I was always doing stuff like that to show them they didn't own me."

"But they did," I said.

"They did," he responded. "Past tense."

I nodded now, too.

"The agency completed its background checks on you a few weeks after our engagement."

"Yet you never told me you knew."

Sebastian's eyes landed squarely on mine and stayed there, almost daring me to look away. I didn't.

He took my hand, stroked it. "I figured there was a reason," he said. "Some wall you had put up. I didn't know if I should pull it down." He paused. "Did you not trust me enough to tell me?"

"It wasn't that. Like I said, I was embarrassed, especially about the arrest. I thought it would lower your impression of me. Mostly, it was a dark time in my life—it was a version of myself I didn't want to revisit."

Sebastian studied me. He gently pushed my hair back from one side and pulled it over the other. Then he asked questions about Billy and me, questions he said he'd wanted to ask me for a while. I told him about my fear of losing Billy, my willingness to put up with so much, the favor asked from his brother Mick, my arrest, and finally Billy's rejection and the humiliation of that.

"You could have told me," Sebastian said.

"It was sordid."

Sebastian shook his head a little. "Not to me. And not compared to what I've seen."

We were both quiet for a moment.

"Your past didn't make me love you less. It made me love you more," Sebastian said. "In part because I had a past, too. I was ashamed, too. All journalists hate the use of reporters by the CIA to gather information."

"Why?" I said. "Weren't you just helping your country?"

"Maybe. *Maybe*. They never tell you, the reporter, the result of what you did for them. They never tell you if the information you gave them proved something or disproved another or maybe even led to someone's death."

Sebastian stopped then as if hearing his words and surprising himself. He glanced around. I wondered how he saw the room differently than I did. I only saw the group of people holding signs to the right of the arrivals hallway, and a man who strained his neck, holding a huge bouquet of flowers.

I sat back, wordless, wanting to hear more.

"The worst part, and the reason that reporters and news agencies hate it," Sebastian said, "is because it gets other reporters, ones who aren't working for the CIA, into trouble. The suspicion about reporters has led to people being kidnapped and tortured."

I tried to take it all in. I tried to assimilate this new information, assessing it as if it were going into a database, piece by piece.

"What are you thinking?" he asked.

"You just said that my past made you love me more."

He nodded.

"And I return that," I said. "I think this…" I waved my hand near him "…what I've learned about you, well, it fleshes you out in my mind. I always thought of you as just Sebastian, star journalist."

Again, his eyes were downcast.

I told Sebastian that his shame was misplaced. It would be different if he had understood the potential ramifications to other journalists. He hadn't. He really had believed, deeply inside himself, that he was helping.

"There's no shame in that," I said. "Please, please don't see shame in it. Because if you do…" I shrugged. "What am I supposed to do about the thing I feel guilty about?"

He grinned. "I missed you."

I grinned back.

"No, like, I *missed* you," he said.

I knew he meant more than just while he had been arrested, more than the time he had been gone on that trip.

"Me, too," I said.

We both took in big breaths.

Then he leaned in toward me. The world whirled with memories, but mostly with him. Now.

"Okay?" he said.

"Okay," I said.

And he kissed me. His warm, wide mouth touched gently onto mine. Then with increasing firmness, fervor.

After a moment, as if shy and surprised, we pulled back.

I sighed. He did, too.

"Your Dogger is in the car," I said.

"Let's go, then."

We walked outside. The town car driver, a guy named Trent, was standing outside the car but his head was visible in a back window, apparently petting the dog. Then Baxter's head appeared over his shoulder.

"Dogger!" Sebastian said.

The driver stepped back and Baxy saw Sebastian. He yelped, then scrambled, jumping out the window.

Sebastian laughed and grabbed him.

The driver opened the door with a flourish of his arm. He smiled at Sebastian, but didn't seem to recognize him. The news of Sebastian's arrest and release (as well as being the dad of Superdog) had been publicized but only with mentions of his status as a journalist. Very few people but me would ever know he worked for the CIA. Sebastian and I had shared all of our pasts now.

I got in the car and my ex-husband followed with our dog.

"Where are we heading?" Trent said, getting in the front seat.

Sebastian smiled at me. "Let's go to the dog park?"

I nodded, and we drove toward another new life.

* * * * *

Acknowledgments

Thank you to Amy Moore-Benson, my agent, my sometimes cowriter and, most important, my friend.

Thank you to Emily Ohanjanians, who shepherded and edited this book and made it shine. Thanks to Donna Hayes, who shepherded a publishing house and a ton of authors over the years. Thanks to everyone at MIRA—Craig Swinwood, Loriana Sacilotto, Margaret Marbury, Tara Parsons, Stacy Widdrington, Ana Luxton, Diane Mosher, Stefanie Buszynski, Evan Brown, Erin Craig, Stephen Miles, Emily Martin, Reka Rubin, Don Lucey, Michelle Renaud, Lisa Wray, Alex Osuszek, Andi Richman, Gordy Goihl, Dave Carley, Erica Mohr, Darren Lizotte, Fritz Servatius, Anne Fontanesi, Nick Ursino, Matt Hart, Audrey Bresar, Gaëtan Bélair, Nanette Long, Laurie Malarchuk, Heather Foy, Aideen O'Leary-Chung, Marianna Ricciuto, Julie Forrest and Carly Chow.

Finally, thanks to everyone who consulted on this book, including Anne Szatkulski, for answering questions about campaign offices and photo shoots, the team at Lincoln Park Dog and Cat Clinic, and Dr. Suma Raju of Roscoe Village Animal Hospital.

And for all the people who passed through Jonquil Park while I was writing this book, thanks for sharing your dogs with Shafer and your time with me. (And hey, thanks, Shafer!)

National Bestselling Author
Dakota Cassidy

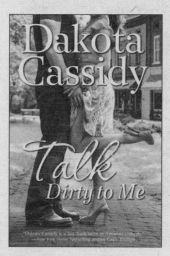

Notorious mean girl Dixie Davis is flat broke and back in Georgia. Her best—make that only—friend, Landon, has thrown her a lifeline from the Great Beyond. Dixie stands to inherit his business…*if* she meets a few conditions:

She's got to live in Landon's mansion.

With her gorgeous ex-fiancé, Caine Donovan.

Who could also inherit the business.

Which is a phone sex empire.

Wait, *what?*

Landon's will lays it out: whoever gets the most new clients becomes the owner of Call Girls. Can Dixie really talk dirty *and* prove that she's cleaned up her act?

Available now, wherever books are sold!

Be sure to connect with us at:
Harlequin.com/Newsletters
Facebook.com/HarlequinBooks
Twitter.com/HarlequinBooks

HARLEQUIN® MIRA
www.Harlequin.com

MDC1619

REQUEST YOUR FREE BOOKS!

2 FREE NOVELS
FROM THE ROMANCE COLLECTION
PLUS 2 FREE GIFTS!

YES! Please send me 2 FREE novels from the Romance Collection and my 2 FREE gifts (gifts are worth about $10). After receiving them, if I don't wish to receive any more books, I can return the shipping statement marked "cancel." If I don't cancel, I will receive 4 brand-new novels every month and be billed just $6.24 per book in the U.S. or $6.74 per book in Canada. That's a savings of at least 22% off the cover price. It's quite a bargain! Shipping and handling is just 50¢ per book in the U.S. and 75¢ per book in Canada.* I understand that accepting the 2 free books and gifts places me under no obligation to buy anything. I can always return a shipment and cancel at any time. Even if I never buy another book, the two free books and gifts are mine to keep forever.

194/394 MDN F4XY

Name   (PLEASE PRINT)

Address   Apt. #

City   State/Prov.   Zip/Postal Code

Signature (if under 18, a parent or guardian must sign)

Mail to the **Harlequin® Reader Service:**
IN U.S.A.: P.O. Box 1867, Buffalo, NY 14240-1867
IN CANADA: P.O. Box 609, Fort Erie, Ontario L2A 5X3

Want to try two free books from another line?
Call 1-800-873-8635 or visit www.ReaderService.com.

* Terms and prices subject to change without notice. Prices do not include applicable taxes. Sales tax applicable in N.Y. Canadian residents will be charged applicable taxes. Offer not valid in Quebec. This offer is limited to one order per household. Not valid for current subscribers to the Romance Collection or the Romance/Suspense Collection. All orders subject to credit approval. Credit or debit balances in a customer's account(s) may be offset by any other outstanding balance owed by or to the customer. Please allow 4 to 6 weeks for delivery. Offer available while quantities last.

Your Privacy—The Harlequin® Reader Service is committed to protecting your privacy. Our Privacy Policy is available online at www.ReaderService.com or upon request from the Harlequin Reader Service.

We make a portion of our mailing list available to reputable third parties that offer products we believe may interest you. If you prefer that we not exchange your name with third parties, or if you wish to clarify or modify your communication preferences, please visit us at www.ReaderService.com/consumerchoice or write to us at Harlequin Reader Service Preference Service, P.O. Box 9062, Buffalo, NY 14269. Include your complete name and address.

LAURA CALDWELL

32932	CLAIM OF INNOCENCE	___ $7.99 U.S.	___ $9.99 CAN.
32666	RED, WHITE & DEAD	___ $7.99 U.S.	___ $8.99 CAN.
32658	RED BLOODED MURDER	___ $7.99 U.S.	___ $8.99 CAN.
32650	RED HOT LIES	___ $7.99 U.S.	___ $8.99 CAN.
32501	THE GOOD LIAR	___ $6.99 U.S.	___ $8.50 CAN.
31373	FALSE IMPRESSIONS	___ $7.99 U.S.	___ $9.99 CAN.

(limited quantities available)

TOTAL AMOUNT	$ _____
POSTAGE & HANDLING	$ _____
($1.00 for 1 book, 50¢ for each additional)	
APPLICABLE TAXES*	$ _____
TOTAL PAYABLE	$ _____

(check or money order—please do not send cash)

To order, complete this form and send it, along with a check or money order for the total above, payable to Harlequin MIRA, to: **In the U.S.:** 3010 Walden Avenue, P.O. Box 9077, Buffalo, NY 14269-9077; **In Canada:** P.O. Box 636, Fort Erie, Ontario, L2A 5X3.

Name: _____

Address: _____ City: _____

State/Prov.: _____ Zip/Postal Code: _____

Account Number (if applicable): _____

075 CSAS

*New York residents remit applicable sales taxes.
*Canadian residents remit applicable GST and provincial taxes.

HARLEQUIN® MIRA®
™ www.Harlequin.com

MLCA0814BL